sandstone
slate
pumice
fluorite
quartz
gneiss
obsidian
marble
limestone

SAMANTHA
HANSEN
Has
ROCKS
in Her
HEAD

SAMANTHA HANSEN Has ROCKS in Her HEAD

by
Nancy Viau

Schiffer Publishing Ltd
4880 Lower Valley Road · Atglen, PA 19310

Other Schiffer Books by the Author:
Beauty and Bernice, ISBN: 978-0-7643-5580-6
Just One Thing!, ISBN 978-0-7643-5162-4

Originally published by Abrams Books/Amulet Books, New York
BIGSTOCK Image: by Yaalan
BIGSTOCK Image: by clearviewstock.
Library of Congress Control Number: 2018956621

Edited by Kim Grandizio
Designed by Jack Chappell
Cover design by Danielle Farmer
Cover illustration by Julia Mills

Type set in Adobe Garamond Pro/Fink/Segoe Script

ISBN: 978-0-7643-5692-6
Printed in China

Published by Schiffer Publishing, Ltd.
4880 Lower Valley Road
Atglen, PA 19310
Phone: (610) 593-1777; Fax: (610) 593-2002
E-mail: Info@schifferbooks.com
Web: www.schifferbooks.com

To my parents, for instilling
in me a love of nature.
And to kids everywhere who
remind me to enjoy it.

CONTENTS

1. A ROCKY START 9
2. DOUBLE TROUBLE 17
3. SKELETONS, BURROS, AND A HORSESHOE 27
4. IT'S MY SISTER'S FAULT 36
5. NOT READY FOR SCHOOL 46
6. A RESCUE MISSION 61
7. YOU CALL THIS A CAVE? 72
8. A PRETTY GREAT IDEA 85
9. THERE'S A BULLY ON THE PLAYGROUND 91
10. NOT SORRY 100

11. **PARTY TIME** 106

12. **A TALENT THAT SHINES** 116

13. **ON OUR WAY** 124

14. **HOOVER DAM JAM** 137

15. **BARELY INN** 146

16. **IT'S A HIKE, ALRIGHT** 155

17. **LOST OR FOUND?** 165

18. **CLOUDY, WITH A CHANCE OF TODD** 174

19. **CHANGE** 179

ACKNOWLEDGMENTS

I'd like to extend my deepest gratitude to the readers who loved the first edition of *Samantha Hansen Has Rocks in Her Head*, and who encouraged me to find a way to keep this title in print.

Thank you to Schiffer Publishing for reissuing the story. Now, a whole new decade of young scientists can be inspired by Sam's love of our planet.

And finally, a big thank you to all the teachers out there who show kids that science is just as entertaining as television or a smartphone.

1

A ROCKY START

I WASH MY FAVORITE ROCKS in the bathroom sink, wipe them with Mom's frilly purple towel, and put them in an egg carton. The egg carton smells a little bit like eggs, but that doesn't matter. Nobody will notice once they see my rock collection. I've been hard at work trying to make this science project *ab-so*-lutely special. I want to get an A+—my first A+ for fourth grade.

I love my rock collection! I already know the name of every rock, but nobody else does, I'm sure. So I'm going to make cool-looking labels. I run to get markers and notepaper from Mom's desk. If she asks me, I'll tell her I'm borrowing them. But I'm not planning on giving them back.

Then I hear the yell. It's coming from our bathroom.

"*Aaargh!* Samantha Hansen! Get your stupid rocks out of here. I want them gone. Like, now! They're in my way."

It's just Jen, my big sister. Jen likes to boss people around. Since I'm the only other kid in the house, I'm a perfect target. So what if I'm a ten-year-old? I don't need a boss who's fifteen. I'd trade her for a turtle if I could.

"Rocks can't be stupid!" I yell back to Jen. "They don't have brains."

I rush to the bathroom because I want to make sure Jen didn't touch my rocks. I peek inside the egg carton. They were touched alright! In four giant steps, I'm in Jen's room. She has her orange nail polish open, and it's stinking up the whole place. Jen paints her pointy pinky nail and doesn't bother to look up.

"Jen, my shiny rock—it's quartz, by the way—is upside down. And this skinny one that looks like blurry plastic—my mica—is in the wrong spot. What did you do? Huh? Shake the carton like a can of hairspray? Use a piece of clay to smooth that gelled-up frizz on your head? See if my glow-in-the-dark green rock makes decent eye shadow? Huh? Huh?"

"Sam!" Mom calls from down the hall. "Stop yelling. This house isn't big enough. Can't you speak nicely to your sister?"

I don't have an answer to Mom's question. I'd probably be nicer to Jen if she were nicer to me.

Jen does her eye-roll thing—she's good at this—and grins like a chimp. My sister loves it when I get in trouble and she doesn't. "Close the door on your way out. *Puh-leeze*," she says with a smirk.

I flip her light switch off, then push the door shut with my foot. Really hard.

"Hey, I can't turn my light back on. My nails are wet. *Mommm!*"

I ignore Jen, hide in my room, and hope Mom thinks the wind slammed her door. Mom doesn't like door-slamming. She says it shakes the shingles off the roof, but she imagines that.

I know that my mouth sometimes has a mind of its own. Words spill out like lava from a volcano. A *loud* volcano. And my body sometimes follows my mouth. These things just happen.

I can't help it. Well, most of the time I can't help it. I walk to my bedroom door and kick that one shut, too. There sure is a whole bunch of wind in here.

The phone rings. I lay my rock collection gently on my pillow and answer it. It's Kelli, my best friend.

"You wanna sleep over tonight?" she asks. "I promise I won't make you look at fashion magazines or try to curl your hair or anything. And we can play that game you love—Archeology Quest. You know, the one where the archeologist has to find missing keys to unlock the world's treasure. I think it's *bor*-ing, but whatever. We can stay up late. Tomorrow is Sunday, so we can sleep till noon."

"Sounds fun, Kell!" I say. "But I might not be on my mom's good side right now."

"You yelled at your sister again, didn't you?" Kelli says. "What happened this time?"

Kelli knows me pretty well. We've been friends since kindergarten. It all started when I was away at camp. A new family had moved into the empty house to the right of us, and Mom was excited to tell me that she saw a girl who might be my age. I couldn't wait to meet her. There wasn't a single girl my age within eleven blocks! As soon as I got home, I saw Kelli zip by on her fancy bike. I spied her curly brown hair peeking out from under her helmet, her girly clothes, and very clean shoes, and I thought: *No way. She's not like me at all. We'll* never *be friends.* But Kelli stopped over that day, and even before she said "hi," she spit out, "I don't wear T-shirts. Or sweatpants. And I don't like playing sports or digging in the sandbox. And, oh, I don't eat spaghetti, bologna, or tuna." I giggled when I heard Kelli say she didn't eat tuna. I don't like tuna, either. Then Kelli smiled back at me and said, "You wanna come over to my house and play?" We've been friends ever since. Best friends. I think I only got mad at her ten or twenty times.

"Kell, hold on a minute." I listen at my door. No Mom footsteps. There's dead silence, except for the gurgle-whooshing sounds echoing from the dishwasher.

I plop on my plaid bedspread and put my ear back to the phone. "Yep, I yelled at Jen. Who else? Holy cannoli, Kell. My sister is the most annoying thing on this planet. There was some door-slamming, too. But maybe my mom is too busy to ground me."

"You hope," Kelli says. "Well, ask her about a sleepover anyway. Maybe you could empty the dishwasher or take out the trash. Be sweet. Supersweet."

"Sure," I say. "I'll talk to you later."

I press the button that ends the call. I can't let Jen get to me for the rest of the afternoon. I should probably tape my mouth shut. And maybe tie my shoelaces together, just to be safe. I wouldn't want my feet kicking anything they're not supposed to.

Five minutes later, Mom knocks and walks into my room.

"Sam, you're grounded," she says. "For hollering and for slamming doors."

"But only for a while, right?" I ask, knowing I'm not going to like the answer. My eyes start to leak and I swipe away one fat drop that rolls down my cheek. "Kelli wants me to sleep over tonight. And I haven't slept over at her house in weeks. Nobody but Kelli ever invites me for sleepovers. I *have* to go."

"No sleepover, Sam," Mom says with her eyebrows pushed together. "You've got to learn to stop yelling at your sister."

"Even if she yells first? That's not fair, Mom."

"You're the loudest, Sam."

Mom reminds me to count to ten every time I feel like exploding. Counting is supposed to keep me calm. It doesn't always work.

I remind Mom that I try. Every day. A huge sigh escapes from me. *Pshoo*. I'm happy to see Mom's eyebrows return to their regular spots.

Then Mom says something I cannot believe.

"I've decided that the three of us could use some quality family time—a vacation. Not long ago, Uncle Paul and Aunt Frankie and their kids went to the Grand Canyon. He said the airfares from Philadelphia to Las Vegas aren't too expensive. And, if that cheap-o brother of mine and his twin hooligans can get through a family trip, so can we. What do you think, Sam? Can you and your sister travel together without killing each other? The canyon's not that far from Vegas. We can rent a car there and have a little road trip. It'll be an adventure."

"Are you serious?" I ask. I have to ask because that word—vacation—has never been part of Mom's vocabulary. *Ever*. My eyeballs are the size of sunny-side-up eggs, I'm sure.

Mom smiles, but only halfway. "We haven't been on a real vacation since, well . . . you know. You don't remember the trip to Disney World, do you? You cried the entire flight. We got you settled down in the hotel, but you cried again when we entered the park. Goofy and Mickey Mouse scared you. Maybe you never imagined them to be so large. Dad swept you up in his arms and carried you all day long."

While Mom tells this story, the color drains from her face. She looks plain and much older for a few seconds. Like her prettiness has been sucked out.

That face is the reason I never ask about Dad. I have a teeny memory of him, but there is so much more I want to know. I love it when Mom tells me about when we were a whole family. Whole things are *way* better than parts. Parts of things end up in fractions, and I *ab-so*-lutely don't like fractions.

"Anyway," Mom continues, "it would be nice for you and me and Jen to get away. Just us girls. But you have to learn to put a lid on that temper of yours."

The Grand Canyon is a dream come true for a rock scientist like me. I'm going to need a very tight lid. And quite possibly, a different sister.

DOUBLE TROUBLE

MOM INVITES AUNT FRANKIE and Uncle Paul for dinner. They come over a lot because they live next to us. Mom wants to go over vacation stuff with Uncle Paul. She needs directions to the Philly airport and directions to the Grand Canyon. How could anybody miss that place? It takes up four-thirds of Arizona, I think.

Having family here is good news and bad news. The good news is that I get to be ungrounded. I can go outside and collect more rocks for my project while I'm waiting for dinner to get on the table. And if I'm outside, that means I'm absent when Mom looks for somebody to set that table. The bad news is that my twin cousins, Ana and Casey, want to do everything I do. They follow me around. Everywhere. Even to the bathroom. But I close the door before I get busy in there.

I find my rock-digging supplies—a cracked beach pail with a lopsided handle and a mini sand shovel. On the way out the door, I grab my green spiral notebook with the 3-D picture of Earth and drop it into the pail.

Our backyard has grass (sort of), dirt, some branchy climbing trees, and a soft place where the evergreens close out the real world and the pine needles make a carpet. I begged Mom to let me have my bedroom in that magical forest tree place. She said, "We'll see." That was three years ago.

In the front yard there's a long, bumpy dirt driveway. I don't have any driveway rocks in my collection, so I start there. I'd love to find a piece of basalt.

I take out my notebook, flip to a clean page, and write:

DRIVEWAY ROCKS

1. Basalt

Basalt is kind of an ugly, dull gray, but it's cool because it looks like bugs have made holes in it the same way moths once made holes in our blankets.

2. Gneiss

I've never actually seen this rock, but it must be nice because it's pronounced *nice*.

3. Quartz

My library book called *Put This Rock in Your Pocket* says quartz is everywhere, so I bet it's here in my yard.

I sit on the driveway, scoot the loose dirt around with my shovel, and see a piece of coal sticking out. I add that one to my list, too.

4. Coal

Coal is great because it comes out of the ground already clean and shiny. But I wish it came in a color other than black. Red coal would be better.

"You wanna play movies?" Ana asks, skipping in circles around me.

Ana loves this game. It's where she sings part of a song from a movie she has seen over and over again. I'm supposed to sing the rest. For all the years we've been cousins, Ana doesn't get that I am not a singer.

"No, Ana," I say. "I don't want to play that dumb game. And can you please skip somewhere else? You're stepping on some coal I want to dig out."

Ana stops skipping. She pushes out her bottom lip so far a pigeon could perch there.

"C'mon, Ana. Don't cry. Just move. Please?"

Ana doesn't budge.

"You don't want to get dirt on your yellow patent leather shoes, do you?"

Ana doesn't look worried. She sings, "Hi, ho! Hi, ho! It's . . ." Then she twirls around and points to me.

“Ana.” I sigh. “Jen is better at this game than I am. Why don’t you ask her to come out and play?”

Ana sings again. “Hi, ho! Hi, ho! It’s off to . . .” She twirls again and this time she points to me with both pointer fingers.

It’s useless. If I don’t play, Ana will keep going and going. Three-year-olds are like that. They’ll drive you nuts if you let them.

“Work. I. Go,” I say, not singing.

“What’s the rest?” Ana asks.

“I don’t know,” I say. “But I *do* know that your song is right. I have to go to work.” I bang the flat part of my shovel on the ground. It makes a loud *slap* and driveway dust goes flying.

“Mommy!” Ana screams. “Sammy pushed dirt on me. My *purty* dress is durrrteeeeee!”

Ana runs away to find Aunt Frankie. This happens all the time, so I’m not worried. Aunt Frankie never hollers at me. “Ana has a habit of bending the truth,” Aunt Frankie says. That’s a nice way of saying that Ana is a big fat liar.

I try to dig out the coal, but I need a sharper shovel. I head for the garage, and in there I see a huge one, the kind

Mom uses to move dirt in and out of the garden. It's exactly pointy enough, but it's leaning against the back wall and out of my reach. I have to climb over a box to get it. But when I do, I fall in!

The box is almost empty, except for the nine-thirds of it that I take up. I crawl out and peek inside. A purple folder is the only thing in there. On the front is a long word that somebody wrote in black block letters: LANDSCAPING. It's not Mom's handwriting. Or Jen's. And inside the folder there are papers with lists and diagrams.

TYPES OF GRASS

1. Kentucky bluegrass
2. Rough bluegrass
3. Perennial ryegrass
4. Fine fescue
5. Tall fescue
6. Red fescue

TYPES OF SOIL

1. Sand
2. Silt
3. Clay

And there are a bunch of other lists. Every list has something to do with our lawn.

TYPES OF FERTILIZER

OK, I don't actually need to read about the different kinds of animal poop.

There's a drawing in the folder, too. It's like a map I saw in my social studies book that showed how the Romans got water to their city. Oh, I know what this is! It's a sketch of where someone thinks we should have sprinklers. We don't have sprinklers, so I guess this never got done. Maybe that's why our grass looks like hay.

I go through the other loose papers and see:

THINGS I NEED TO FIND OUT MORE ABOUT

1. How to get rid of moles and voles without killing them
2. Environmentally safe pesticides
3. How to build a fancy-schmancy swing set for my girls♥

I love the teeny heart at the end of number three.

Wait. I know who made these notes. I think.

I flip through the rest of the papers. And freeze. *Ab-so*-lutely freeze. There's a photo of Dad next to a lawn mower—the same lawn mower Uncle Paul uses to mow our lawn now. Dad is smiling. It's a smile *way* bigger than any smile I've seen in any photo Mom has (except for maybe Mom and Dad's wedding picture). He looks like he's having a really good time. And what is he holding in his hand? He's holding *this* purple folder. Holy cannoli! I don't believe it! Dad was a note-taking list-maker, just like me!

I tuck Dad's papers carefully into the folder, put everything back in the box, and shuffle back down the driveway. I'll think more about Dad's lists later. Right now, I need to get to work.

I dig out the coal in five-sixtieths of a minute flat and plop it in my pail. Farther along the driveway, I spy a sparkly rock. When I pick it up and squeeze it, it breaks. I'm not sure what this soft, mystery rock is, but whatever it is, I now have two pieces. I turn around to put them in my pail, and notice that my coal is gone!

I see the other twin, Casey, running around the yard. "Hide-and-seek, hide-and-seek," she says.

I can tell right away that Casey has something to do with my missing coal. She comes over and gives me a big hug. "Sammy, I hided your rock. You wanna seek it?"

I reach back to pull Casey's pudgy arms from around my neck. Her hair smells like baby shampoo. Aunt Frankie must use it on the twins' hair. It reminds me just how young they still are. "Casey, I don't want to seek it. Can you just get it for me? It's a special rock that I need for school. For a science project."

"I'll give you a clue," Casey says. "It's buried."

On days like this I miss having just Jen around. At least Jen doesn't bug me to play with her. I'm forced into doing the hot/cold game with Casey so I can figure out where she's buried my coal. I don't get warm until I'm halfway around the garage twice and end in the same place I started.

"Now you're hot," Casey says as I walk down the driveway. "Hot. Hot. Hotter. You're boiling hot!"

I'm at the bottom of the driveway. Two more steps, and I'll be out in the street.

"Fire, fire, fire!" Casey calls.

"Casey, you're too good of a hider. I give up. Tell me where my piece of coal is."

Casey giggles. "It's in there, silly," she says.

Now I know where to look. Casey "buried" my rock in our mailbox.

It's going to be a long night, I'm sure.

3

SKELETONS, BURROS, AND A HORSESHOE

SUNDAY MORNING I WAKE UP early to finish my rock collection. I want to add my driveway rocks and rearrange everything in alphabetical order. I have to get this project done today. It's due tomorrow.

"Sam!" Mom calls. "Come join us for breakfast. We're having Strawberry Coco Swirly Whirl birthday cake with our cheese omelets. There's cereal here, too, if you'd rather have that."

I hear Mom singing "Happy Birthday." It's not my birthday or Jen's. Mom always sings that song. Sometimes she makes up new words. When I get to the kitchen, I hear:

Happy birthday to me.
Happy birthday to you.
We may share a birthday,
But my gift better be new.

And we eat a ton of birthday cake. Usually two or three times a week. It shows up at breakfast, lunch, dinner, or snack time. We never have it for dessert. It's gone by then. We sometimes have meatloaf for dessert.

Mom works for the Sunny Funny Card Company. Her job is writing birthday cards. Mom says that the birthday song and cake keep her in a cheery mood and help her think of new things to write about. Mom is her happiest when she's making cakes. I don't think this is strange, but every once in a while when a friend—not a best friend—comes over, they let me know right away how weird they think Mom is. I don't explain that Mom's birthday happiness is a huge cover-up—she just acts this way so the birthday cards turn out funny and she can make money. Mom has sung a thousand birthday songs and made a thousand cakes since Dad died. And they've all turned into ideas for Sunny Funny birthday cards. But none of them really make her happy.

I keep a list of favorite cakes in my head:

CAKES I WILL EAT WITHOUT COMPLAINING

1. Surprise Cake (comes in a bunch of flavors)

I like most of these, but her Chocolate Surprise Cakes are the best.

2. Devil-May-Care Angel Cake

This one is one-half dark chocolate and eight-fourths fluffy vanilla.

3. Pineapple Inside-Out Cake

Mom's Pineapple Inside-Out Cake is much better than the Pineapple Upside-Down ones I've eaten in restaurants. Mom puts the pineapples on the inside, bottom, and top!

4. Bunny Yum Cake

This is really Carrot Cake, but we like to call it Bunny Yum Cake. It's filled with carrots, but I can't taste a single one.

5. P, B, & J Cake

This cake doesn't look like a cake at all! It looks like a peanut butter and jelly sandwich on yellow bread.

I fill up a bowl with cereal and Mom cuts me a slice of cake. The swirls are fancy, but today the smell of cake makes my stomach flip-flop. It flip-flops a lot these days. Mom says they're growing pains, but I think it's because I'm finally sick of cake. Especially Strawberry Coco Swirly Whirl Cake. Most kids would love a treat like this in the morning. Not me.

"Mom! Not strawberry again! This is our third strawberry cake this week! We just had Strawberry Banana Merry-Go-Round Cake last night when Aunt Frankie and Uncle Paul were here. And last Wednesday, you packed Strawberry Shortstop Cake for my school snack. Pink! Pink! No *way* am I putting anymore pinkish food in my mouth." My words pop out like microwave popcorn. But louder.

"Ugh." Jen moans. "I am *so* not awake enough for this noise."

"Sam, count to ten," Mom says, calmly. She gives me that I'm-going-to-ground-you-again look.

"But Mom! Can't I skip the cake? Can't I—"

And then a picture of the Grand Canyon flashes before my eyes. I take a deep breath and count out loud so Mom and Jen can hear me. "One, two, three . . ." I think about three kinds of rock formations, four sedimentary rocks, five igneous ones, sixty metamorphic ones, seventy striped ones, a hundred brown ones. What number am I on? It's too hard to count! I open my mouth and shove in two spoonfuls of cereal, followed by two forkfuls of cake. Eating is probably a good way to shut myself up. I can't yell if my mouth is stuffed with food. I'm dying to eat only the cereal, but a few yells might sneak out through the flakes. I *will* get to the Grand Canyon! Even if I have to eat ten thousand strawberry cakes to get there.

I toss my plate in the sink just as Kelli strolls in through the back door. She winks at me and smiles at Mom. "Hello, Mrs. Hansen. How are you today? Gee, it smells yummy in here." Kelli isn't sure if I'm ungrounded or not. That's why she's being extra nice.

"Oh, it's just strawberries, but thank you, dear," Mom explains. "Don't you look spiffy today? Is that a new hairstyle?"

Kelli beams. "Sure is. I got it out of a magazine. It's supposed to go with my naturally round face and olive complexion."

Jen nods like she knows exactly what Kelli's talking about. I have no idea why Kelli believes having skin like an olive is a good thing.

"You ungrounded?" Kelli asks me.

"Yep. Wanna help me with my rock collection?"

"Sure," Kelli says, "but I don't know squat about rocks. And if they're dirty, I'm not gonna touch them."

We leave the kitchen birthday party and go to my room. Pink cake is one thing, but if Kelli hangs around Jen any longer, they'll be talking fashion till the sun goes down. Kelli doesn't have an older sister, so she borrows mine now and then. If it were up to me, I'd trade my sister for Kelli's two older brothers in a heartbeat.

"Sorry I couldn't sleep over last night, Kell," I say to her. "But guess what? My mom says if I keep a lid on my temper, she'll take me and Jen to the Grand Canyon."

"That big hole in the ground?" Kelli asks. "I've been there. I only got to shop in one souvenir store! Just one! Can you imagine? And I had to hike forever—like maybe five or ten hours—before my parents let me go shopping. And after I went in, I couldn't wait to come out. There were rocks, and books about rocks, and crystals that grew on rocks. *Bor*-ing. The store did have some nice cushiony benches in there, though. I sat next to a cute boy who bought a book with a skeleton on the cover. He told me that each chapter was about a missing hiker. Yikes. You don't want to get lost in that place, Sam. They'll never find you."

"I won't, Kell. Don't worry. And I won't be shopping either. I want to explore! That canyon is the biggest chunk of sedimentary rock on the planet. And I want to see some fossils. And I want to ride a burro to the bottom, and . . ."

"*Eeeww*. Burros? Those dumb animals *stink*. And they walk extremely slow, so you have to smell them a long time. They *clip-clopped* past me when we were on the trail. An enormous burro pooped right by my shoe. It was major gross."

I giggle at the thought of burro poop near Kelli's bright white sneakers. She won't walk her own poodle, Snooky, because of the poop factor.

Kelli finds some felt in my craft box. "Hey, this silver piece matches that rock over there," she says. "Won't it look great if I stick a square of colored felt under each rock? I'll cut out a piece to match each one. Won't that be gorgeous?"

I smile. Kelli is definitely artsy. I have to admit her idea will make my collection look like an A+ project.

Two hours fly by. Kelli goes home to work on her own collection for school. I should probably help her with her labels, but I don't have a clue how to label hair accessories. Or how hair accessories fit in with our science unit called The Living Earth.

For the rest of the afternoon, I read about the Grand Canyon on the computer. I knew it was beautiful, but there's a lot I never really understood. Like how the river got way down there, and how the whole canyon got formed from that river. And most importantly, how many kinds of rocks are there. But thanks to the internet, I now know these things.

I click on the Tourist Information link, and see something I cannot believe. There's a part of the canyon that doesn't have anything to do with rocks. It's a piece of glass shaped like a horseshoe that sticks out over the canyon. In midair! Builders built it so people can step out over the canyon. *Way out* over the canyon! It might be fun to walk on that horseshoe and feel like you're on a cloud. But that horseshoe thing looks shaky to me. And scary. What if someone jumps on it and the glass cracks? Or what if I eat so much cake that I weigh five hundred pounds by the time of our trip and I walk on that horseshoe and it breaks? In half.

I don't think I'll mention the horseshoe to Mom. She might make this part of our "adventure." I like my feet on rock-solid ground. I'll be able to see the canyon just fine.

IT'S MY SISTER'S FAULT

I TUCK MY ROCKS IN FOR THE NIGHT by covering each one with its matching piece of felt. I kiss them, close the lid of the egg carton, and find a comfy place for them on my stuffed-animal shelf. I arrange my fluffy friends around the collection. Now they'll have something fun to look at while I'm sleeping. Sandy, my lobster, Bob the beetle, and Wally, my huge walrus, all love rocks and rocky places, I'm sure.

"Ace, you're coming with me," I tell my favorite penguin. I can't sleep without Ace by my side.

I like to read before I go to bed, but I've done so much reading on the computer today that my brain feels foggy. For quiet time tonight, I decide to work on notes for the Grand Canyon trip. My brain is never too foggy for making notes. Writing down notes helps me unjumble the thoughts in my head. And I have a lot of thoughts wandering around in there about our trip. I sit in bed and prop up my pillow, but not before I reach under it to get my green spiral notebook. Most fourth-grade girls keep diaries under their pillows. I don't need a diary because I don't have anything to write about boys. Especially about boys in my class. But I do have lots of important scientific things I want to remember. Like the names of the driveway rocks I found this weekend, and other stuff. On the first page I have:

THE PLANETS AND THEIR MOONS

1. Earth: Moon

2. Mars: Phobos and Deimos

3. Jupiter: Europa and about 78 other moons I can't remember

4. Mercury: no moons

5. Venus: no moons

I have to look up the rest, but I learned something by making this list. They are not all called the Moon! On another page I have:

STUFF ABOUT BUTTERFLIES

1. Metamor-something-I-can't-spell

2. Egg

3. Larvae

4. Poopa (or is it pupa?)

5. Adult

I like bugs. A lot. I'd like to have a bug for a pet someday. Or maybe some other pet I can actually walk around the block.

I skip over these pages and start a new list:

THINGS I WANT TO LOOK FOR ON THE GRAND CANYON TRIP

Underneath, I list the rocks I want to find:

1. Limestone

Is it lime green?

2. Sandstone

I should be able to find sandstone rocks. Ten-tenths of the whole place is made of that.

3. Marble

I read about a Marble Canyon on the internet earlier, so I bet I'll find some marble rock in the canyon somewhere.

4. Shale

Shale there is mostly reddish orange. It's what makes the canyon so beautiful.

5. Schist

I'm not sure what schist is, but it's a boring blackish color. At least that's how it shows up on my computer.

I remember that computer picture. It showed the major rock layers of the canyon. I should draw it in my notebook! I make a flat-topped rock—a plateau—and write "limestone" on the very top. I draw another not-very-straight line under limestone and label that part "sandstone." And then I add some shale. And more limestone. And more sandstone. I'm at the bottom already and there's no room for schist!

BOOM. Boom. Squeak.

This is a noisy house.

BOOM. BOOM. Boom. Squeeeeak.

I know why I'm having trouble drawing!

Squeak. Squeak.

"Jen!" I holler. "Your music is driving me crazy. I can't do my notes! Can't you turn your speakers down? Can't you turn them *off?*"

Jen probably cannot hear me. I cross the hall to her room.

"Scientists need quiet!" I yell over the hip-hop song.

"Get a grip," Jen says calmly. "I'm not turning anything down. Or off."

"Yes, you are," I say, diving for her cell phone. Jen tries to tackle me, but I'm faster than her. And *way* louder. We stay there for a second with both our hands flattened on her thin, bedazzled phone. "Jen, let go!"

Jen pushes my hand away. I lose my balance. And plop on the floor. "Ouch!" One of Jen's hair-clippy things has bitten me on my butt.

"Now that's not my fault," Jen says. She turns her music up louder.

I holler over the booming squeakiness, "If you don't turn your music off, I'm gonna yank—"

"Sam, let go of your sister's hair!"

Mom sure is fast. She must sit and wait around for me to lose my temper. And I am trying very hard to be good. I have to remember to get mad at Jen in a much quieter way.

"What's going on, girls?" Mom asks. "You know I'm under a lot of pressure to get this batch of birthday cards done before tomorrow morning. If I don't make my deadline, you can kiss our Grand Canyon trip good-bye. What's the fuss about?"

"Sam's being weird again," Jen answers. She slips over to her bed and pretends to do homework.

I send her invisible darts from my eyes. "I am not weird. Your music is."

I make my face smiley before turning back to Mom. "Don't make me count to ten. I'm done yelling. I just need quiet so I can make notes for our trip. Jen's music makes me mess up. And a scientist's notes have to be neat. I asked her nicely at first, but she didn't hear me because her music is *so* loud." My smile disappears when those last two words pop out. And they pop out more in Jen's direction than Mom's. "Jen, you should go live with Uncle Paul and Aunt Frankie. Ana and Casey need an older sister. I don't."

Jen is shaking her head. She's not saying a word. She's acting like she has nothing to do with this fight.

I have to fill in the quiet. "Mom! If Jen weren't around, I'd be sweeter. I'd be sweeter than Zucchini Berrilicious Cake. I'd never . . ."

Mom looks confused. What is she mumbling? Her pointer

finger is pointing to my room. And she's holding the fingers of her other hand up one at a time. Is *she* counting to ten? How is she planning to do that on a single hand? I don't think it's a good idea to stick around and find out. I shuffle off to my room. And that big wind—the wind that comes from my foot—slams the door shut again.

I chew some bubblegum to keep my mouth busy. There might be more words that want to escape. I take my spiral notebook, find a new page, and write:

TYPES OF FOSSILS I KNOW

1. Trace: footprints, eggs, animal nests, or poop!
2. Mold
3. Cast

I only remember the fossil names, not what they actually look like. We studied this in school, but I missed it. Probably because I was very worried about a loose tooth that day. It doesn't matter. I'll add more to these notes the next time I bring home my science book.

I want to find a bunch of fossils in the Grand Canyon. Mom says I'm a great finder. Whenever she loses something, she pays me a dollar to search the house. I find it in a minute, of course. At the canyon, I wouldn't care what kind of fossil I'd find, but a dinosaur fossil would be best. A *live* dinosaur that gobbles up my pain-in-the-butt, trouble-starting sister would be even better.

JEN-EATING DINOSAURS

1. Tyrannosaurus rex

One bite. That's all it would take. Gulp.

2. Velociraptor

Jen is on the track team and she runs fast. But this meat-eater runs faster.

3. Muttaburrasaurus

This dinosaur is a plant-eater, and Jen's not a plant. But I *ab-so*-lutely *love* its name. And it'll mistake my sister for a plant if she has on her green dress, I'm sure.

5

NOT READY FOR SCHOOL

I CAN ALWAYS TELL it's Monday morning. Monday is my favorite day to sleep in. Saturdays and Sundays I'm up before the sun. But on Monday, my eyes are superglued shut.

"Sam, it's seven o'clock!" Mom calls. "Time to get ready for school."

I moan. I learned that from Jen. When Jen grows up, she should be an actress and star in a movie where she gets to moan and whine for hours. Jen could win an award for Best Drama Queen Whiner in Hollywood. And then she'd move out and live with the rich and famous and have everything her way.

A few yawns later, I climb out of bed. To tell the truth, I don't mind going to school. Mrs. Montemore is my fourth-grade teacher at Centertown Elementary, and so far, I like her a lot. In first grade, I had old Mrs. Milkens. Everybody had to shout out answers because if Mrs. Milkens didn't hear you, you got a red check in her grade book. I never had much trouble with the shouting thing, but a couple of quiet, shy kids almost ended up repeating first grade. I had a funny teacher in second grade. His name was Mr. Butts. It was a good thing Mr. Butts came with a sense of humor. In third grade, I had three teachers: The first one lasted two months. She left around Halloween to have a baby. The second teacher decided to become a nun and nobody knows why. By the time we got Ms. Ziegler, I was ready for anything. Ms. Ziegler gave me the creeps. She picked her nose when she thought the students weren't looking.

But Mrs. Montemore will go down in history as my all-time favorite because she likes science as much as I do. Well . . .

almost. She has this not-so-fun habit of sneaking scientific words into our spelling list. Last week, she added the planets and made us write them in their order from the sun. "My Very Earnest Mom Just Saved Up Nine Pennies," Mrs. Montemore said. "The first letter is the first letter of the planet. The 'M' in 'My' stands for Mercury, the 'V' is for Venus, and then of course there's Earth, Mars, Jupiter, Saturn, Uranus, Neptune, and Pluto."

That same day, I helped Mrs. Montemore out by telling her that scientists can't make up their minds about the number of planets in our solar system. Some say Pluto is not a planet at all. Some say it's a *dwarf* planet. Some say there's another planet, Planet X! I won't ever forget Planet X. I can spell that one.

I look out my window and decide it's sunny enough to wear summer clothes. Fall is here, but it still gets hot in the afternoon. I don't like being uncomfortable, so I step into my shorts and pull on a T-shirt. It's brown and blue and has a great-looking mountain on it.

"*Mommm*," Jen says the minute I get to the kitchen. "Check out what Sam's wearing. She dresses like a boy."

"I do not," I say. "Who ever said mountain T-shirts are only for boys? Huh? Look at your hair, Jen. It has an orange stripe." I say this a bit too loud.

"Sa-man-tha," Mom says. "Pipe down."

"I like my shirt!" I spit out. But then I snap my mouth shut. When Mom turns my name into three separate syllables, I know I better listen. And her eyebrows are pushed together again. Come to think of it, they've been stuck like that for a couple of weeks. Maybe Mom really *does* need a vacation.

"Sam, your sister is right. You do need to change. That shirt has a hole in it on the top of Mount Everest. I thought I sewed that last week."

I can't win. Jen can dye her hair and Mom does nothing, but I say something that's true—loud, but true—and I get hollered at? It's not fair.

Jen grins. She *ab-so*-lutely loves to be right. She tosses her flippy hair, sits down, and puts a teeny piece of toast between her glossed-up lips.

"Jen, you and I will talk later," Mom says. "And for the record, I'm not fond of your orange hair, either. If you're going to dye it, at least make it a decent color."

I smile but it doesn't show up on my face. I hope Mom talks to Jen about sticking her nose where it doesn't belong. But Mom's been so busy lately, I bet she forgets about it. That thought makes me want to be sick smack on top of Jen's striped head. I lean over and open my mouth. I know I can't make myself throw up if I'm not sick, but Jen probably doesn't. Wait. What am I doing? I have to stay on Mom's good side. And this isn't how to do it.

"Aw, c'mon, Mom," I say. "Please can I keep this shirt on?" I'm very proud of myself because I am much quieter than I was a few seconds ago. "This hole is special. It's supposed to be there. It's where climbers found a cave. I *love* this T-shirt! Don't make me change it!"

Next door, Kelli's poodle starts to yap because I guess I woke him up. Snooky doesn't like to get up much before lunch, I'm sure.

Mom's hands are on her hips, but I keep going. Words fly out of my mouth like a remote-control race car that speeds down the street, only I'm not about to run out of batteries anytime soon.

"Mom, trust me. It's the best T-shirt *ever*. No one has a shirt this great. I cut that hole so . . ."

"Sam, count to ten. Take a deep breath—in and out—and count. Then find another shirt." Mom turns on the mixer and the bizzle-buzzing sounds fill the whole kitchen. She belts out another "Happy Birthday" tune:

Happy birthday to me.
Happy birthday to Sue.
Calm down right this minute,
Or I'll throw cake at you.

I get the message and look for some cake to eat to shut me up. The dried-up pink leftovers from yesterday will have to do. Chew. Chew. One and two. I won't yell anymore. Three and four. Grand Canyon . . . fossils that come alive. Four and five. Five and six? Pick up sticks? I've lost count again!

I chug-a-lug my milk and take off down the hall. But not before my elbow jabs Jen's arm. Slightly. Almost not at all. My elbow does that sometimes. It comes out of nowhere and has a mind of its own. Like my mouth. And like my foot.

"*Mommm*," Jen whines. "Did you see that?"

In my room, I pull my T-shirt over my head and throw it on floor. I try on seven others and think about another list:

WHY I'D TRADE MY SISTER FOR A TURTLE

1. Turtles are not annoying.
2. Turtles are quiet.
3. Turtles mind their own business.
4. Turtles do not care what you wear.
5. Turtles do not dye their hair.
6. Turtles like rocks.

When I get to T-shirt number eight, I stop and put that one on. It has a truck-driving praying mantis on it. That bug's face is so cute I almost forget how mad I am at Jen. I scoot the rest of my shirts into one big pile, make a wrinkled opening in the sleeve of the mountain T-shirt, and tuck my stuffed bear, Teaberry, inside. On a piece of scrap paper I write:

BEAR CAVE
DO NOT TOUCH
BEAR BITES!
HE ESPECIALLY LOVES TO BITE
TEENAGERS WITH ORANGE HAIR

Mrs. Montemore would love that I recycled my T-shirt into a toy. Mom probably won't be too thrilled that my clothes are crumpled on the floor.

I catch the bus just in time and sit in my regular seat next to Kelli.

"My sister thinks I dress like a boy," I tell her.

Kelli shrugs her shoulders up to her dangly earrings.

"Do I?" I say using my outdoor voice—the voice the bus driver doesn't want to hear *inside* her bus.

I scare Kelli awake, I think. She isn't a big talker first thing in the morning. She needs at least five or ten blocks before her eyelids stop looking droopy.

"Shhh!" Kelli whispers. "The bus driver is looking at us in her mirror. You're gonna get us in trouble."

I give Kelli a quiet nudge. I pinch my lips together and tilt my head at a goofy angle. And make my eyes huge. "Well . . .?"

"I heard you," Kelli says. "You just don't like girly clothes—like skirts and dresses and stuff. You would look nice in a skirt. *If* you liked them. Look at mine. It's new. Isn't it pretty? See the adorable kitty cats on the side here? And I have a matching headband, but I forgot that today, and matching socks, but they're in the wash. And I *love* this peachy color. And you know what? This skirt comes in white with puppies, too. Ling has that skirt . . ."

Kelli is very awake now. If she were a radio, I'd turn her off.

Before long, I skip into Mrs. Montemore's room. I hang up my jacket and backpack in the closet and go to my seat. I sit in the back of the room where all the good kids sit. The bad kids sit in the front where Mrs. Montemore can keep an eye on them.

There are a lot of chatty kids back here this morning. They're hanging around two long tables that were set up over the weekend. On the tables I see: Kelli's hair-accessory collection, Gregory's leaf collection, Kristin's shell collection, Matt's chicken-feather collection, Kat's nut collection, and Ling's rock collection.

Wait! Rock collection? Oh, no! Ling copied me? Then it hits me. Ling couldn't have copied me. I forgot to bring my collection in today!

Everybody is gushing over Ling's rocks . . . big time. Ling painted her egg carton and coated it in gold glitter! Why didn't I paint my carton like that? It would have covered up the eggy smell!

"That chunk of granite looks like our kitchen countertop," Jimmy Star says.

"Is that real chalk?" Joanie Benner asks.

"Wow, that rock is shiny and silvery. You could make gorgeous jewelry with that. It could be a charm on a bracelet," Kelli says.

I stare at Kelli with a scrunched face. "You can't like her collection more than mine, Kell," I whisper. "She's not your best friend. I am."

I walk up to Mrs. Montemore's desk. "Mrs. Montemore," I say. "Umm, I left my collection at home. It's a rock collection. And it's *so* much better than Ling's. My gerbil pushed it under the couch. And that's why I forgot it."

I am almost not fibbing. Much. I *had* a gerbil. His name was Cody. And there is a couch in the real story. Cody escaped last year, and I couldn't find him for days. I kept telling myself that he'd be OK and that I'd find him soon. But I didn't find him. Jen did. I can still hear the drama queen scream, "Dead mouse! Dead mouse!" She'd moved the couch when her friends came for a sleepover, and Cody was under there. He was very still. *Ab-so-*lutely dead. Mom wouldn't come near him, so I had to scoop him up with a cooking spatula. On my way out to the backyard, I cried so many tears I almost dropped him on the deck. I made a grave for Cody in Mom's flower garden. To this day, I can't see a daffodil without bawling. I should have looked harder for Cody when he was lost. Mom is wrong. I'm not such a great finder.

My furry friend is gone, and my eyes leak as I remember him. I don't like to think of him as permanently dead. I can't possibly explain that to Mrs. Montemore.

Mrs. Montemore looks at me funny. "Please sit down, Sam. Just bring in your collection tomorrow."

Whew! Mrs. Montemore is nicer than the ice-cream lady—the one who gives us seconds for free if the temperature crawls up close to a hundred.

"And," Mrs. Montemore adds, "I hope you'll bring your gerbil to school someday. I'd like to see him."

"OK," I mumble, as I picture myself digging Cody out of the garden. I'm pretty sure Mrs. Montemore doesn't really want to meet Cody in his condition.

I don't say a word while the kids talk about their collections. Kelli does a good job explaining how hair accessories fit in with science.

"They're plastic," she says, holding up some clawlike pincher clips. "So we don't need to knock down any trees to make them."

I bet her mom told her what to say. Her mom is a lawyer and is good at making up stuff. At least that's what Mom told me once.

Kat tells the class how nuts turn into trees. She drew a beautiful poster that shows which nut goes with which tree. Kat is supersmart, I think.

Ling is up next. She points to her rocks and talks in a show-offy voice. "This rare rock is only found in South America," Ling says.

No it's not. I can't keep quiet any longer. My hand rockets to the ceiling like I'm not even attached to it. "Ooh, ooh, Mrs. Montemore," I spit out. "Quartz isn't rare. It's found everywhere. And Mrs. Montemore, do you see? Some spots in Ling's carton don't have any rocks." Then I turn to Ling. "Couldn't you find any to fit in there?"

I smile at Mrs. Montemore. She's probably thrilled that I pointed out those empty spots. Ling's collection shouldn't get an A+. It's nice, but B+ nice.

"In *my* collection," I say, "I have a big piece of quartz—bigger than Ling's—and a holey piece of pumice, some driveway coal, some mica, and pyrite, which is like gold, by the way."

The class oohs and aahs when I say "gold." I can talk about rocks forever. And I don't have to make up a single word.

"And I have a really shiny one that might be a diamond, two soft ones that I call my mystery rocks, and . . ."

"Stupid rocks," Richard Frey says. "Samantha Hansen has rocks in her head."

"Do not!" I snap back at him. But everybody is already laughing.

Mrs. Montemore claps her hands.

Clap. Clap. Clappityclapclap. Clap. Clap.

This is her special signal that means *Be quiet now, or else.*

"Samantha, we'll look forward to hearing more about your collection . . . when you bring it in tomorrow."

Mrs. Montemore sure knows how to shut a kid up. I feel my cheeks get warm. I bet everybody notices how great my face matches Ling's reddish rocks.

At the end of the day, Mrs. Montemore hands us a blue paper. On the top it says:

FIELD TRIP PERMISSION SLIP

On the rest of the paper there are a bunch of blank lines that parents must fill in. Without reading it, I tuck my permission slip in my homework folder. I don't want to lose it. I lost a permission slip in second grade when I put it in my desk and it disappeared. I almost didn't go on the Philadelphia Zoo trip! And I lost a permission slip in third grade, too. I put that one safely in my jacket pocket, but it got eaten by the washing machine, I think. I almost didn't go on the Walking Tour of Philadelphia trip! Both times the teacher had to call home so Mom could come to school and sign a new slip. Permission slips are a pain in the butt.

Mrs. Montemore waves blue paper. "Class, don't forget, next week we are going to Slippery Stone Cave. You'll learn some fun facts—like how stalactites are different from stalagmites, how a cave is formed, and what types of rocks and minerals are in caves in the eastern part of the United States."

My insides turn to mush. Slippery Stone Cave? A real cave! Mrs. Montemore mentioned this trip before, but I forgot about it. Probably because my mind has been busy with the Grand Canyon. But this field trip will be *ab-so*-lutely cool. I should find my cave book tonight—the one called *Fun Spelunking*. Mrs. Montemore needs my help. I can tell already. She's calling our trip a *field* trip. She should call our trip a *cave* trip. Mrs. Montemore would never survive without me, I'm sure.

6

A RESCUE MISSION

WHEN I GET HOME FROM SCHOOL, I grab an apple and wave to Mom. She's sitting in her office next to the kitchen. She likes her office there. The cake smells go to her brain faster. Mom is typing on her keyboard to the beat of pretty violin music that comes from her speakers. "Happy Birthday" sounds strange when an orchestra plays it.

Other than the sounds coming from Mom's office, the house is quiet. I peek in Jen's room. She's not there. She's probably hanging out with Timmy after track practice. I don't get why she likes that freckled boy. He looks like an alien.

My rock collection is still sitting on the hall table where I left it this morning. I hope I remember to bring it in tomorrow. Mrs. Montemore might act like the mean mail lady instead of the nice ice-cream lady if I forget it two days in a row.

In my room, I zip through my math homework because I don't like math and it doesn't like me. We work on fractions a lot in fourth grade, and no matter how hard I try, I don't understand parts of things. Just like I don't understand why my family has to be a *part* and everybody else's family gets to be a *whole*. I wish Dad were still here, so we could be a whole *whole*. And not only that, Dad could explain this whole fractions thing to me. But I don't know that for sure.

I do know that I'm leaving the last part of my homework unfinished. I can't divide a square cake into eight-sixteenths. Since we have so much cake in this house, I should know how to do this. But all of our cakes are round.

I call to Mom as I head toward the front door. "I did about eight-eighteenths of my homework, and I'm going over to Kelli's for a while."

"Wait a minute," Mom says, catching up to me. "How was your day?"

"It was OK," I say. "I'll tell you about it later."

Mom smiles and sings me out the door:

Happy Monday to you.
Why do you look so blue?
We'll talk more at dinner.
Don't you know that I love you?

"Be back at six, Sam," Mom says, and blows me a kiss.

Outside my front door I wave to Uncle Paul, who is mowing his lawn. Ana and Casey are coloring with sidewalk chalk. They don't see me, and I scoot off to Kelli's house.

Before I knock on Kelli's door, I see that the two-story house on the other side of Kelli's—the Turners' old house—is still for sale. I wonder who will move in there, and if I'll be away at camp when they do. I hope it's a fourth-grader who loves earth science as much as I do. Maybe supersmart Kat will move there. Since she likes nuts so much, she'd love this yard. It's filled with acorns! We'd collect them, plant them, and make a whole forest of oak trees. She would become my second-best friend, I'm sure.

Kelli comes running from the back of her house. "I'm playing with my dolls on my swing set," she says. "Clarissa wants to go to a party. But Megan wants to go shopping. I'm pretending they're having a big fight and Clarissa wants to run away."

I'm not thrilled that I might be playing with dolls, but I follow Kelli anyway. She has the best swing set in the neighborhood. It has a three-story clubhouse built into it, a rainbow slide, and a rock-climbing wall.

When we get there, Kelli's older brothers, Alan and Danny, are sitting on top of the swing set. They're squatting there like monkeys on a branch. They're not allowed to be doing that, I think. Alan has Clarissa by her hair, and Danny has Megan upside down. They've tied plastic grocery bags to the dolls like parachutes and are about to launch them off the swing set!

"Alan! Danny!" Kelli hollers at them. "What are you doing?

Look at my dolls' hair! I spent all morning making them look beautiful."

"Clarissa decided she wasn't a party girl," Alan tells Kelli. "She ran away to join the Air Force. She wants to be a parachuter."

"And Megan missed her, so she followed her," Danny smirks.

The boys think this is funny. Kelli does not. Kelli looks like she's about to cry. "Put my dolls down, you beasts!" she says louder.

"Get ready to bombs away!" Danny shouts.

"Ten, nine, eight . . . ," Alan counts.

Kelli is not giving up. "I want my dolls!" She's very upset, I can tell. I have to do something! I run over to the rock-climbing part and jump up and down. The whole swing set shakes.

"Hey, Sam, knock it off," Alan says. "You're gonna make us fall."

"Go, Sam! Go, Sam!" Kelli cheers.

Both boys drop the dolls ever so carefully into Kelli's arms, so they can hold on tighter. Then they swing down from the top and leave us alone.

Kelli gives me a hug. "Thanks, Sam. You saved Clarissa and Megan."

"Kell," I say, "I have a question. When your brothers were doing that, you were really, really mad, right?"

"Sure was."

"But you didn't lose your temper. Or get too loud. How'd you do that?"

Kelli shrugged her shoulders. "I don't know. Maybe it's because my brothers have been teasing me forever. I'm just used to it. And if I would have started a fight, my mom would have made me go inside. I didn't want that to happen."

Kelli is very thoughtful to think ahead like that.

I swing on the swings while Kelli gets the plastic bags off Clarissa and Megan and puts them in their travel case. Then we do front-flips on her gym bar. Kelli tries to teach me how to do a backflip. She starts by sitting on top of the bar and holding on. Then she falls backward and tucks her head in so she doesn't bump it, and she somehow ends up with her feet on the ground. But I can only do the sitting-on-the-bar part.

"I'm happy being a front-flipper," I tell Kelli.

We play for an hour before it's time to go inside.

Back home, Mom has dinner ready. Jen is eating over at a friend's house. I'm glad I don't have to put up with her. I've had a hard day, and she started my hard day this morning.

"So, how's my girl tonight?" Mom asks.

"Well, I forgot to bring my rock collection to school," I tell her.

Mom puts a plate down in front of me and gives my shoulder a gentle squeeze. "I saw the egg carton on the table and wondered about that. If you called me, I would have brought it in."

"Mrs. Montemore says I can bring it in tomorrow. It's a really great rock collection—much better than Ling's. Trust me. Mrs. Montemore will love it. Hey, guess what? We're going on a field trip next week. To Slippery Stone Cave! You have to sign a permission slip."

"Let's not lose this one, Sam," Mom says, chuckling.

Mom knows me pretty well. She remembers what happened with my last two permission slips. She serves me a small slice of Chogurt Cake—cherry yogurt cake—with lots of ham and baked beans on the side. Chogurt Cake is hot pink. And so is ham. Even baked beans are pink. Well, pinkish red. A sigh escapes from my mouth. *Pshoo.*

Mom hears me. "No comments about dinner. I'm warning you."

"Holy cannoli, Mom. Pink, again?" I slump into my chair. "And you know how I feel about Chogurt Cake. It's not even close to being a favorite. In fact, it makes me want to choke, and . . ."

"Sam, before you bubble over, count to ten like we talked about."

I'm not sure about the bubbling thing, so I count to ten to myself while I shove in a few bites. All that flipping this afternoon has made me hungry.

Mom keeps talking. "I remember a time when you loved the color pink—you were two and wore nothing but pink. If I tried to dress you in any other color, you had a fit. And there was that day in nursery school when you had to make a Christmas card out of red and green paper. You gave Ms. Linda a tough time because you wanted to make yours out of pink paper."

Mom goes on to tell me four more pink stories. My favorite one is about a pink toy laptop I got for my second birthday. I remember it had a fake screen. If I wanted to change what showed up, I turned a handle and the paper rolled around to a new picture. The paper was always getting jammed, and I'd cry until Dad fixed it. But one day, Mom said that Dad wasn't here to fix things anymore because the "man upstairs" needed him to work on a very important computer. Dad had to go help him. I was OK with this until I turned three and noticed we didn't have an upstairs. That made me mad. Then Mom told me the truth: Dad had gotten really, really sick and died. I don't like that truth. Neither does Mom. That's why the color drains out of her face when she talks about him. And that's why I never ask questions about him. Even though I want to.

I wonder what I'd talk to Dad about if he were here. That would make a good list, I think:

DADDY-SAMANTHA CONVERSATIONS

1. Pets: gerbils, fish, cats, AND dogs

I bet Dad would let me have a dog. Did he have a dog when he was my age?

2. Sports: surfing, swimming, diving

I don't like sports much. But I'd try a water sport. Wait. Would Dad want me to do a land sport? I hear lots of kids brag about how their dads are soccer coaches. Would Dad be a soccer coach? Oh, no! Would I be a soccer player instead of a scientist?

3. Dancing: hip hop, ballet, close-so-your-checks-touch dancing

Once, when Mom tried to show me that last kind, she laughed and said I had two left feet, just like Dad. It meant I stepped on her toes. Did Dad go around stepping on ladies' toes?

4. Piggyback rides

I've never had one, but I would ask Dad to show me how it's done. Kelli tells me dads give the best piggyback rides.

5. Bedtime stories

Every night before I go to sleep, I'd read Dad a story. Or he'd read one to me. He'd kiss me and hug me (twice!) and make my covers nice and smooth. Dads are great tucker-inners, I'm sure.

I'm thinking that I won't have trouble keeping the lid on my temper. I'm a little sad tonight. And tired and hungry.

And I secretly love ham.

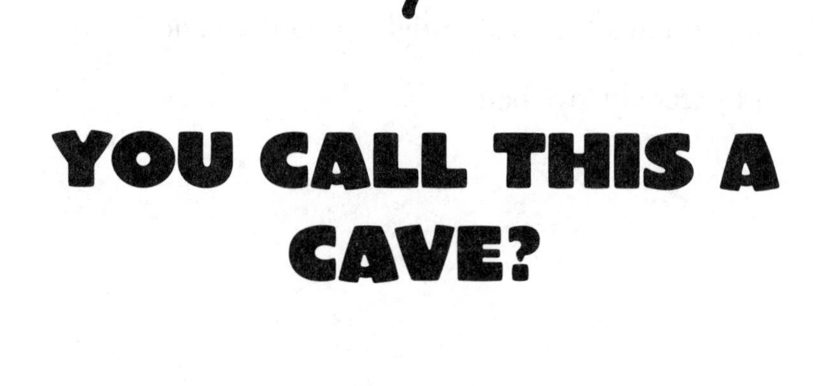

7

YOU CALL THIS A CAVE?

THE WEEK FLIES BY, and it's Tuesday—the day of the class trip. I can't wait to see Slippery Stone Cave. I've looked up a ton of cave facts on the internet. I've been so busy that Jen hasn't gotten on my nerves. Much. Alien Timmy is her boyfriend now, and she yakkety-yaks on her cell phone to him all the time.

"Mom, did you sign the paper from Mrs. Montemore?" I ask. "She has to have it today or else I can't go." I'm thrilled that I remembered the permission slip this time.

"Yes, Sam. It's been on the table for days," Mom says. She kisses the top of my forehead, turns me around, and gives me a teeny shove toward the table. Then she hums her way to her office. By the time she gets through the door, her humming has turned into a song—a song that's probably on its way to being a birthday card today.

Happy birthday to you.
Happy birthday to you.
You're now fifty years old,
So get a new hairdo.

I grab the blue paper and run to the bus stop. I don't mind one bit that Mom has signed her name in purple icing.

We don't stay in school long. Another bus picks us up and we are off to a real cave! I sit up front, next to Mrs. Montemore.

She looks tired, and I know I can help her wake up.

"Mrs. Montemore, how long does it take to get to Slippery Stone Cave?"

"It's a half-hour drive, Samantha," Mrs. Montemore says, yawning.

"Thirty whole minutes?" I unzip my backpack. "We can play Travel Bingo. I have some cards in here somewhere."

"Let's just save our energy," Mrs. Montemore says. "We have a long day ahead. Maybe you should relax and think about what you want to do for the talent show this Thursday evening."

Talent show? Oh, that's right. Now I remember. But doesn't Mrs. Montemore know? I don't have a talent. Unless she counts being able to make a U-shape curl out of your tongue. But I nod to my favorite teacher anyway, and lay my head against the window. What should I do in the show? If rocks were real, and could sing, I could sing along with them and be a *rock* star! Now that would be a funny talent. I wonder if I could do something with rocks . . . I'll have to think hard about this.

In a couple minutes, I'll ask Mrs. Montemore about the grade I got on my collection. When I brought it in a few days ago, she gave me that special teachery look. I thought it was an A+ look, but it could have been an A- or a B+ look.

We bump out of town and across the hilly roads of Pennsylvania. The leaves on the trees are trying hard to keep their green color. By the middle of October, they will turn yellow, red, or orange, and the air will smell earthy like the mud on my shoes. By Thanksgiving, the cornfields will be chopped down, the tractors will be parked in the barns, and the land will look lonely. I don't like that look very much.

To keep myself busy, I take out my notebook and write:

TREES I KNOW AND WHAT COLOR THEIR LEAVES ARE NOW

1. Sick-a-more: brownish yellow

I wish I knew how to help sick-a-more trees. They must have a weird disease that makes their trunks look like camouflage.

2. Poplar (or is it popular?): yellowish gold

The popular trees grow together in a group, I'm sure.

3. Oak: goldish red

4. Maple: reddish orange

I peek over the seats to see why we've slowed down. There's a horse and buggy up ahead. We must be in Amish Country. Wherever it is, it *ab-so*-lutely doesn't look like cave country. Caves are big holes in tall, brown mountains. How can a cave be near here?

My eyes feel heavy. Why am I sleepy? I went to bed last night after dinner. I didn't want to take the chance I would fight with Jen and get in any trouble. But then early this morning, a rooster cock-a-doodled a very annoying cock-a-doodle. It was just Ren, Matt Matlack's new pet. I bet Ren is still mad because Matt plucked a feather out of him for his feather collection. Ren can cock-a-doodle louder than any rooster I've heard. Probably because Matt lives across the street from me, and Ren's roost is in the front yard.

Even though it was dark, I got up because I was excited about our school trip. I could have used more sleeping-in time. But I can't fall asleep now—they may forget about me and leave me on the bus. I'll miss the stalactites and stalagmites. And I want to find out if snotties are in Slippery Stone Cave . . . or maybe they are snot*tites* ... I saw them in a book. I wonder if . . .

Somebody is pushing my shoulder back and forth.

"Sam! Wake up!"

Kelli is standing next to me. "What are you doing in my bedroom?" I ask, squinting through my eyelids.

"We're at Slippery Stone Cave, sleepyhead," Kelli says. "You slept the whole way. I could hear you snoring from my wheel-hump seat near in the back. You snore louder than both my brothers together."

"Where? What? The last thing I remember is looking out the window and seeing the Amish buggy. What did I miss? Where's the cave?"

Mrs. Montemore calls from the front of the bus. "Class, when you get off the bus, line up. We need to walk up four sets of steps to the cave's entrance."

I wave both hands in the air. "Ooh, ooh, Mrs. Montemore. We must be in the wrong place. Steps aren't part of caves."

"Samantha, these steps make climbing easier for visitors."

"Oh." I'm not sure what to say about the climbing thing. I was right. Mrs. Montemore wouldn't know a good cave if she fell into one.

"Steps to a cave? Is this a kiddie park?" I whisper to Kelli as we ramble out of the bus.

Kelli smiles at the steps. She's in love with them. Her brand-new, superclean, light-up sneakers won't get near a glob of dirt. And there isn't a single piece of poop in sight.

We start climbing, up and up. I walk and step. And walk and step some more. Stepping this many steps is *way* harder than I thought. I don't have steps in my house because everything's on the first floor. It's a ranch-style house. No steps. Huff. Puff. Not. Huff. One. Puff. Step. Puff. These steps make me breathe heavy like the wolf in the *Three Little Pigs* book. Where is the top?

Four-quarters of an hour later, I see it—a bright yellow sign in capital letters that says:

SLIPPERY STONE CAVE ENTRANCE

It *is* a big hole! Right in the middle of nowhere. Right here in the middle of this hill at the top of a whole bunch of steps.

"Hello, my name is Susie," a woman with a squeaky voice announces. "I am your guide today. Before we enter the cave, there are some rules."

I catch my breath and squiggle my way next to Susie. "Don't break off the pointy rocks inside," I tell Susie and the class. Sometimes my very loud voice comes in handy.

"Yes, yes, thank you. That's an important rule," Susie says.

"And watch where you walk. It's slippery. Because if this is a really good cave, there is water around here somewhere."

"OK, that's another rule . . ."

"And watch out for bats," I add. The boys will be happy that there might be bats in here.

"Indeed. You know quite a lot about caves, Miss . . ."

"My name is Samantha Hansen. I really like science. I *ab-so*-lutely love rocks more that anything."

"Yeah, she's a science freak," somebody calls from the back.

"Samantha Hansen has rocks in her head," somebody else says.

The whole group is snickering and making weird faces at me.

"So what if I know more about rocks than any of you?" I say to those mean kids. My voice is loud. It probably echoes past the entrance sign and down the steps.

Susie puts her fingers to her lips and shushes me. I don't pay attention to her. Instead, I stare at the kids in my class. "Who said that about me? Richard Frey, was that *you?* You don't know about caves at all. Caves are filled with cool stuff. Like glow-in-the-dark minerals and slime and limestone . . ."

"Samantha," Mrs. Montemore calls. "Settle down. Let Susie talk."

My mouth snaps shut. It just does that by itself when Mrs. Montemore tells me to do something. Especially if she tells me in front of everybody else. But I have lots more to say to those clueless kids back there. Most of all, that I am *not* a freak.

Without planning it, I hear myself whisper, "One, two, three, four, five, six." I'm thinking that'll work for now because I made it ten-sixths of the way, and that's better than zero-sixths.

Susie explains more rules. "When we first step into the cave, allow your eyes time to adjust to the darkness. Walk in a single file. Don't run. Like Samantha says, the cave floor is slippery. Hold on to the handrails when we climb up and down. Do not push the person in front of you. We will stop at spots along the path. Wait for me to point out interesting things in that area. Do not turn off any light switches you may find hidden in the cave walls. Do not touch, remove, or kick any of the rocks or boulders."

"Did she say lick a rock?" some girl asks. "Who'd lick a rock?"

I chew on my lip because I want to yell out one more rule: Don't ask stupid questions.

Finally, we take our first step into the darkness. There is a slight glow from Susie's flashlight. And there are mini lanterns in the cave's walls. I am in shock at how pretty it is. The rock walls are mostly smooth with many colors mixed in—light brown, dark brown, yellow, white, and shiny gray. A reddish rock that sits by itself on a flat rock shelf reminds me of a ladybug. Another rock on the floor is shaped like a rabbit.

We go deeper and deeper into the cave. Two kids are shaking and holding Mrs. Montemore's hands. These are the same kids who get scared at movie time because the lights are off. They're babies, I'm sure.

"Here is a stalagmite," Susie points out. "It's made from deposits of calcium carbonate. That mineral is carried in the water that drips down from the ceiling. Over time, it grows bigger and bigger."

A real stalagmite? Holy cannoli! It's sharp. I wonder what it feels like. My hand reaches toward it and . . .

"Stop!" Susie yells. "Do *not* touch, please."

I'm secretly glad it's dark because I bet my face is redder than the ladybug rock.

"Now, look up at this stalactite. It's like an icicle."

Some kids giggle and talk to each other. They should listen to Susie.

Susie lifts her chin and frowns over the crowd. "If you're good, I have a surprise for you," she says.

I can't keep a lid on my happiness. "Is it snottites?" I ask. "It has to be snottites, right? Or do you call them snotties?"

"Uh . . . well . . ." Susie isn't answering me very fast.

"Susie, there are snotties here, right?"

"Samantha, I don't know what you are talking about. I've never heard about snottites or snotties before. My surprise has to do with fluorescent minerals."

"But I've seen glow-in-the dark rocks before," I say. "I have ten of them at home."

Susie tilts her head. "You do? How wonderful! Fluorescent minerals are fascinating, aren't they? I'll be showing the class some in this cave shortly. But I'm sorry, Samantha, I don't have any information for you about snottites."

This is a nightmare. Squeaky Susie has to be kidding!

"Sam!" a boy shouts. "Tell us how snot gets in caves!"

Wait. This boy—Todd Kensington—wants *me* to talk?

"I think I saw snottites in a picture once," Todd says. "That cave was darker and creepier than this one. It was in Mexico. All kinds of gooey junk hung from the ceiling. Were they snotties, Sam?"

My mouth takes off like lightning. "I learned about snotties from a library book. And guess what? That cave was in Mexico, too. So maybe you can't find snotties around here. But I'll tell you about them anyway. Snottites are teeny, and they're alive.

And they connect together and grow, and are stringy like snot. But they're not real snot. Snottites eat sulfur, which is strange, I know, but . . ." I stop for a second to take a breath. Everybody is listening. Especially Susie and Mrs. Montemore. And nobody is making weird faces or giggling. Some kids, like Kelli and Todd, are actually smiling at me.

"Totally awesome," Todd says. "Did you ever see pictures of caves that have humongous ledges in them? Some have waterfalls and pools! We could find some pretty cool stuff in those caves. Right, Sam?"

I want to answer Todd. And tell him a whole bunch of other cave facts. But suddenly, I can't remember any more about caves. My mouth is stuck. And my eyes must be, too, because they are staring straight at Todd and not moving. I can't help it. Todd smiles at me some more. He has *ab-so*-lutely perfect teeth. And his eyes are like coal—glassy, black coal. My mouth and eyes may have been stuck, but my mind is going a mile a minute. I'm thinking that maybe, just maybe, I like Todd.

8

A PRETTY GREAT IDEA

WHEN I GET HOME FROM SCHOOL, I find Jen sitting at the kitchen table. She's eating the very last peanut butter cookie. And she's sitting in my seat! Before she sees me, I stop and take a hard look at her. When she's not fighting with me, and she's quiet like she is now, Jen is sort of pretty. Her hair is not orange anymore; she dyed it a regular brown—a little darker than mine. And it's twirled in a circle like a cinnamon bun.

Spiky strands sprout from the back. This stick-up hairdo looks cool. I wonder if she can teach me how to do that.

"So, um, I like your hair," I say. But then I really want to say something else that will make her jump out of my seat. Words pop out of my mouth before I think too hard about this. "Did your lovey-dovey boyfriend dump you yet? Did Alien Timmy go back to the mother ship?" I ask, crossing my eyes.

"Your eyes will get stuck like that," Jen says, not budging. And she opens her fashion magazine to ooh and aah over fall sweaters.

"They will not. I'm not stupid. In fact, I was very smart today at Slippery Stone Cave. I helped out the guide. Big time."

Jen moans. "You went into that ugly, cold chunk of rock? I went there for a field trip in fourth grade, too. Hated it. And when I got home, I smelled like rotten eggs. Like you do now."

"I don't smell!" I say. But I wonder if I do. The cave did have a rotten-egg smell in it. Susie said it was from the sulfur. But Susie didn't know much, I'm sure.

I do a teeny *sniff sniff* on my sleeve. It smells OK to me. Then I do a big *sniff sniff* by Jen's head. "*Ick!* Your hair smells like peaches and watermelon. What are you—a fruit salad?"

Jen almost gives up her seat to go look in the mirror, but Mom walks in. It's good that she does, because me and Jen are just about to have a fight.

"Fruit salad?" Mom asks. "No, we're not having that with the chicken tonight. But I did make a yummy Chocolate Surprise Cake."

This is Mom's second chocolate cake this week. She finally ran out of strawberry cake mix. I love her surprise cakes. And chocolate ones are the best. Once, she filled a chocolate cake with chicken pot pie and called it Lucky Clucky Cake. I wonder what Mom has hidden in her surprise cake tonight.

"You're going to like this, Sam," Mom says, winking. "I talked to a travel agent about our trip. He confirmed what Uncle Paul said about getting a good deal on a flight out west at this time of year. He said he could get us tickets to Las Vegas on Friday morning. I checked with work, and they said I can take off for a long weekend."

"This Friday? We are seeing the Grand Canyon *this week?*" I ask.

"Well, we'll *start* our trip this Friday. We have to drive from Vegas to the canyon, remember?"

I cannot speak. This is a pretty great idea to go to the Grand Canyon so soon. It will be a hundred times better than Slippery Stone Cave. I have to get ready. *Now!*

"Where are you going in such a hurry, Sam?"

Sometimes Mom is *ab-so*-lutely clueless. "I have to start packing this minute."

As I race off, I can hear Jen complaining to Mom. Mom sounds cheery. Jen doesn't. Jen is whining, of course.

"*Mommm*, you're ruining my life. We can't go on Friday. That night is the Spring Fling Dance. Timmy asked me, and I . . ."

I close my door. I don't have time for complainers. I have to put my spiral notebook, trail maps, rock and mineral chart, flashlight, and binoculars into my backpack. I'll put Ace in at the last minute. I won't be able to sleep without my penguin. And right before we leave, Mom will take care of my clothes, shoes, toothbrush, and the rest of that not-so-important stuff.

I can still hear Jen through my door. Why does she care so much about a dance anyway? Can't her boyfriend go without her? When I get a boyfriend, we will skip every single dance. We'll go to the Natural Science Museum instead. If Todd lived on my block, I would tell him about that museum. And I would tell him it's OK if he doesn't ask me to the Spring Fling Dance when we're in high school.

Jen will forget about her boyfriend on the trip. I'll make a scientist out of her yet. Or maybe I can talk her into being a scientist's helper. She can carry my backpack. I'll let her put makeup in it and maybe a teeny mirror and some extra hair supplies. In case I get up the nerve to have her fix my hair like a cinnamon bun.

An hour later, Mom calls me for dinner. She made a cake she called Chocolate Potatolate, but I don't remember eating that surprise cake. There may have been mashed potatoes inside. I do remember the barbecued chicken wings Mom served on pretty salad plates. At least I think that's what was under the chunky white salad dressing.

As soon as dinner is over, I take a quick bath. I don't waste any time playing with my dinosaur soaps. I need to hurry up and go to bed early. Maybe before the sun goes down. If I do this every night, Friday will come sooner. And Matt's rooster better keep his beak shut in the morning. If Ren cock-a-doodles before seven o'clock, I'm *ab-so*-lutely marching over there and having a talk with him.

9

THERE'S A BULLY ON THE PLAYGROUND

I'M DYING TO TELL Kelli my news, but she isn't on the bus. I have to keep it all bundled inside me until recess.

When I do catch up to Kelli, I bubble over. "We're leaving this Friday for the Grand Canyon! And we're taking a plane! I've never been on a plane before. Wait. I went to Disney World on a plane when I was little. But that doesn't count because I don't remember that plane at all. Anyway, I'll see the Grand Canyon soon. Did you know that the whole canyon is made from the Colorado River? And did you know that there's a horseshoe thing that *some* people—not me—can walk out on? And you can see the bottom that's about a whole mile away?"

"Uh-huh, I know," Kelli says, braiding and rebraiding her hair.

"You can walk *into* the canyon, too. How about that? Walk *into* a canyon. You did that, right? That's where you saw the burros. Was it Bright Angel Trail, Kell? Because that's the trail we're going on."

Kelli's not saying much. She's fixing her polka-dotted bows. Kelli is jealous of me, I think. She probably wants to go to the canyon again.

"Hey, Sam," Kelli says, "Let's play Chase-and-Capture with Jules and Hannah."

I say OK because I want to cheer Kelli up. It's not her fault her parents won't take her back to the best place on Earth.

Chase-and-Capture seems like a lot of work today. My legs are sore from the steps yesterday. It's my turn to chase Jules. She is superfast. I try to catch up to her, but my feet move like jelly.

I'm almost by her side when I get tripped.

"Hey, Richard, watch out!" I yell.

"I didn't do anything. You got in my way," Richard says. "Stay off the soccer field."

"You made me fall flat on my head!"

Richard points at the ground and smirks a big fat smirk. "Yeah, well, I bet you can get a closer look at the rocks down there, science freak."

"It was *you* yesterday. You called me that name at the cave! So what if I like rocks," I say jumping up. "At least I don't like chasing a stupid soccer ball around like you do." I turn in a circle and do a fancy soccer move like I would do *if* I played soccer. But when I spin around, I accidentally kick Richard's leg instead of an imaginary soccer ball.

"Hey, you kicked me!"

"Did not."

"Freak," Richard mumbles. His mumble turns into a laugh when he catches up to his friend, Teddy.

I stomp over to those two. "Take that back!" I yell to Richard.

"Will not!" he yells back.

I lean over to Richard so that my nose is about an inch from his. Richard uses his fist to swipe his sweaty, red bangs off his forehead. He looks much tougher up close. But I don't budge.

"Samantha Hansen, come over here this minute!"

Oh, good. It's the recess lady. She's coming to my rescue. She probably saw what happened. And she wants to talk to me about That Kid Richard.

"Go directly to Principal Tancredi's office, Miss Hansen."

"Me?" I ask. "I didn't do anything. It was Richard." Can't she see?

The recess lady turns me so that I'm facing the school. She gives my shoulder a teeny push like Mom sometimes does.

"Move it," she says.

I move it, alright. The recess lady can be pretty scary.

Five minutes later, I'm sitting in a hard, black chair. Principal Tancredi is standing in front of me. I'm scared to look at her face. I stare at her veiny neck instead. Principal Tancredi doesn't like kids, I'm sure.

"We will not allow our tempers to get out of control, young lady," Principal Tancredi says. "We must solve our problems politely. There are rules against bullying in Centertown Elementary. We must obey them."

I don't know why Principal Tancredi is saying "we." She was nowhere in sight. I tell her *we* didn't do anything wrong. And *I* didn't do anything wrong all by myself, either.

Principal Tancredi sways her head back and forth, like an angry dragon. In my mind I come up with a list of dragons that Principal Tancredi looks like:

PRINCIPAL TANCREDI'S RELATIVES

1. Dozer, the fire-breathing dragon with six legs who bulldozes playgrounds, searching for ten-year-olds named Samantha
2. Crazy Copter, the fire-breathing dragon with wings on her head who flies only at night, scaring fourth-grade girls

3. Firecracker, the fire-breathing dragon with veins the size of the Empire State Building who gobbles up rock-loving scientists

I would not be surprised if fire came out of Principal Tancredi's mouth really soon. Maybe she breathes fire on kids when they're sent to her office. Maybe this is why so many kids move out of town. Principal Tancredi makes the recess lady look like a fairy princess.

Thirty minutes later, Mom comes to pick me up. Now I know I'm in big trouble. She is wearing her you're-going-to-get-grounded-forever face.

"Mom," I say in the car. "You'd be mad, too, if somebody tripped you."

"Yes, I would, but I wouldn't be mean, Sam. Principal Tancredi is under the impression you're a bully. How did that happen? When you and that boy had a disagreement, why didn't you count to ten before blowing up and kicking him?"

"I couldn't!" I blurt out. "It happened too fast. Richard started it. He tripped me. And he made fun of me. He called me a science freak yesterday at the cave! And when he said it today, I . . . I . . . " My mouth is moving fast. I'm not sure I can even keep up with it.

Mom pulls to the side of the road. "What happened to keeping a lid on your temper? You've made progress with this at home. You can do it at school, too."

"But I was showing Richard how a soccer kick works, and his leg ended up where my kick was. I didn't mean that . . . so, OK, my foot was there on purpose, but I was copying him because he plays soccer." I stomp my feet on the rubber floor mat a couple times.

Mom turns off the engine and stays quiet. *Ab-so*-lutely dead quiet.

I bang the dashboard. Hard. "C'mon, you have to believe me! *Mom!*"

After a whole minute, Mom says, "When you count to ten, and I am sure you are calm, I will get back on the road. And I will not talk to you again until that happens."

Mom has done this before. I have to sit here and not say a word. I can't breathe. Much. Or let out poofy sighs. It's not easy to do. I'm not good at this at all, and one sigh escapes. *Pshoo!* And another. *Pshoo!*

Mom reclines her seat and gets comfortable.

I decide to practice my will-you-forgive-me face. It's pretty perfect. I've had years of practice. When I show Mom my forgive-me face, she folds her arms across her chest and blinks a very long blink in my direction. Then she lays her head on the driver's side window and stares at a crow in farmer Sorbello's field.

After fifteen minutes, Mom starts the engine and we get moving again. I know I'll get grounded. I probably won't see Kelli for months. She'll probably quit being my best friend. She'll be best friends with that puppy-skirted rock-collector Ling.

"Sam," Mom begins, "I'm not certain you're mature enough for this trip to the Grand Canyon. Perhaps Jen and I will make the trip without you. You can stay with Uncle Paul and Aunt Frankie and your cousins."

What? I'm *not* going to the canyon? My ears must have gotten broken at recess. "You can't do this to me," I tell Mom.

"That would be like taking away my air. I *need* to go. There are rocks there I've been wanting to see since I was *born*."

"Friday is two days from now," Mom says. "Right now, it doesn't seem like the best idea. I hoped that the three of us would go. I wanted to get away and well . . . never mind. What I want is not important. We'll see."

When Mom says "we'll see," it usually means "no." Why can't Mom understand how important this trip is to me? Maybe I can make it up to her. Her fortieth birthday is next month. I can plan an early surprise party. And I'll give her my A- rock collection for a present. An A- is just like an A+ with one teeny line missing. Mom will forgive me, I'm sure.

And since I'm planning stuff, I need to plan how to get even with That Kid Richard. And I want to do it soon before I forget how mad I am. But what can I do? Richard is a tough bully, and I'm just a scientist. Wait. The talent show. I can do something there. I'll need my rocks, my very special ones. It turns out that I do have a talent—a talent for getting even. Tomorrow night That Kid will be very sorry he was mean to me.

10

NOT SORRY

WHEN WE GET HOME, Mom walks me to my room. She tells me I cannot come out until I write an apology letter to Richard and Principal Tancredi. I hear her mumble something about "self-control" and "short fuses" and "lid on your temper." I'm supposed to think about these things.

I'm glad I'm not suspended for three days like the bad kids. Or expelled like the *really* bad kids. But it still feels weird to be home in the middle of a school day. I sit at my desk and wonder what Mrs. Montemore is teaching. We're almost done with our unit called The Living Earth, and the chapter "Rocks and Minerals." Soon we'll be on the next chapter, called "Volcanoes and Earthquakes." Mrs. Montemore shows a movie at the start of a new chapter, and I don't want to miss that. For a minute, I feel very sorry for myself. My eyes leak and tears plop on my homework.

I need to make Mom see I'm not a bad kid. The surprise birthday party will help. A party puts everybody in a cheery mood. I'll make a cake and everything. Mom's "we'll see" will turn into a "yes" this time. I hope. That hope stops the leak in my eyes.

I take out my rock collection and wrap it in yellow polka-dotted tissues—the clean ones, not the soggy ones I just used. I don't have any tape, and I can't borrow Mom's because I can't leave my room. So I use some Band-Aids to hold her present together. I write *Happy birthday, Mom!!!* on the front, and that reminds me: I have to start working on those apology letters.

I know exactly what to put in Principal Tancredi's letter. I am not as afraid of her in writing as I am face-to-face.

Dear Principal Tancredi,

I am sorry I got in trouble today. It won't happen again.

Sincerely,
Samantha Hansen,
the Good Student Who Sits in the Back of Mrs. Montemore's Classroom

P.S. It was That Kid Richard Frey's fault. I hope you sent him home, too.

Now I need to write a letter to Richard. I don't want to apologize to That Kid. Is his mom making him write an apology letter to *me*? Doesn't matter. I can think of a long list of reasons why I don't want to write to *him*.

WHY I DON'T WANT TO WRITE THE HARDEST LETTER OF MY LIFE

1. It wasn't my fault.

2. I don't want to be nice to Richard.

3. Richard won't understand my apology letter because Richard is in the stinky-reader group.

4. Writing a letter isn't nearly as much fun as making notes in my green spiral notebook.

5. A letter is a pain-in-the-butt homework type of thing.

6. I am very well-behaved at all times most of the time, and good girls shouldn't have to write apology letters.

I'm not getting out of this chore anytime soon. Mom will come in and ask to see my letters. I'm thinking she spends fifty-fortieths of her life checking up on me. I plop on my bed and write hard and fast:

Dear Really Mean Richard Frey,

I am NOT sorry I ran on the soccer field when I was playing Chase-and-Capture. It is a free country. We have a free playground. I can run anywhere I want. You should NOT have tripped me. And I know you did it on purpose. Soccer players know what their feet are doing at ALL times. ~~And you are a good soccer player.~~

I cross out that last sentence. It's true, but I don't want it in there.

I am also NOT sorry I kicked you. Because I didn't. It was an accident. Because I am NOT a soccer player. I am clueless about what my feet are doing seven-thirds of the day.

And do NOT call me a science freak ever again.

Very NOT sincerely,
Samantha Hansen,
Earth Scientist

I pace around my room a few times. It's a small room and not made for much pacing. I stub my big toe on my dresser, twice. That hurts! I stop in front of my mirror and count to ten. One, two, three . . . way before number five, I notice my eyebrows are pushed together. I look a little like Mom. But when I get to ten, I look more like Jen. I wonder if there's a part of me that looks like Dad. I could make up a math problem about that. What part of Samantha Hansen looks like her dad? Three-halves, two-halves, or zero-quarters? *Pshoo.* More parts of things. Why are all the important things fractions?

I sharpen my pencil because I used up the whole point on my mad letter. I sit at my desk and write another letter—the real letter that I'll hand in tomorrow.

Dear Richard,

I am sorry. I really and truly thought you tripped me on purpose. And I really and truly did not kick you on purpose.

The end.

Your classmate,

Sam

11

PARTY TIME

ON THURSDAY I run home from the bus stop as fast as a cheetah, because I have so much to do. I'm actually glad Jen is babysitting me. Mom is at the farmer's market buying fresh vegetables that will end up sitting next to our dinner cake some night. This is my chance to get the most important thing on my list done: Mom's surprise birthday party. It's more important than getting ready for tonight's talent show. That's all planned out, anyway. The first thing I have to do this afternoon is to cook a cake. It can't be that hard to do. Mom has done it a thousand times.

There are pictures on the box that tell me what goes in the bowl. I am thrilled that the cake people put them on there!

I open the powdery stuff. It goes *pfluft* and cake dust flies everywhere—especially in the toaster and the coffeemaker. But most of it lands in the bowl. I crack two eggs. I add a third one—because it's pretty fun to crack an egg. Some shells plop in, too, and they don't go away when I mix the pflufty stuff around with a soup ladle. Mom won't care about the shells. I'll tell her it's Shellberry Munch Cake, made from a very crunchy recipe. I take some yellowish oil and try to figure out how much to put in. I'm not sure how to measure one and one-third with a one-cup measuring thing. Don't the cake people know that fourth-graders have trouble with fractions? I pour in enough oil so that the batter looks syrupy, like the batter in the picture.

Then I stop. The last picture shows an electric mixer. Oh, no! I'm not allowed to plug stuff in, especially Mom's electric kitchen stuff. And I don't know the first thing about running a mixer.

"Jen!" I call down the hall. "Are you busy?" I use my lovable-little-sister voice. I know my extra-sweet, soft voice will work. I've used it before when I want to borrow a hair tie.

"What's up?" Jen asks, shuffling into the kitchen. She rubs her eyes. Jen's been napping instead of studying, I'm sure.

"I have a problem," I say, "with this mixer. Can you help?"

"Are you doing another science experiment behind Mom's back?"

"This isn't an experiment, Jen."

Can't Jen tell I'm getting ready to cook? Can't she see the eggs and oil? I count to myself to keep from bubbling over. One, two, three, four, five, six. I need sleepy Jen's help. Seven. Eight. Nine. I take a deep breath—in and out. Ten! I did it! I kept the lid on my temper. "Jen," I say, putting on my helpless-little-sister face, "I want to give Mom a surprise party this afternoon. I want to cook a cake."

"Hey, clueless, it's not Mom's birthday," Jen says. She sticks her finger in the batter and tastes it. She scrunches up her nose. "And you're supposed to say, '*bake* a cake.'"

"I need to have Mom's party now," I say. "But I can't use Mom's mixer."

"She's still upset with you? I heard about the problem on the playground. Boy trouble, huh?"

I nod.

"And now you want to get on Mom's good side, so she'll let you go on the trip."

I nod again. "*Ab-so*-lutely."

Jen smiles a big smile.

"Will you help?" I beg.

"OK," Jen says. "But you've got to make my bed for like, two weeks. Deal?"

"Deal," I say.

"I'll work the mixer for you. And why don't you make cupcakes instead of a round cake? It's easier. If you put foil cupcake holders in the cupcake tins, you won't have to scrub any pans."

That's thoughtful of Jen to think about how much I hate cleaning up. I bet she even sticks around to help me. Jen is also an expert plugger-inner-mixer, and in no time she has my batter looking like the batter on the cake box. When she's done, I pour it into the teeny cupcake places. It's not easy to get that slimy stuff in there. I spill more batter on the outside of the pan than in the foil cupcake holders. The holders are only filled up two-halves of the way, but Jen doesn't whine once.

When the cupcakes are baked, and they're cooling off, I notice something is missing. Icing!

"Jen, do we have any icing—the kind that comes in a can?"

Jen looks in the refrigerator. I dig around in the pantry. There isn't any!

"We can make it from scratch," Jen says. "I'll look up a recipe on that site: Creative Cooking for Clever Cooks. I've seen Mom on it before." Jen reaches across the counter and whips open Mom's laptop. She taps a bunch of keys. "Geez! This idiotic computer isn't working again!" she yells. "If Dad were here, he'd know what to do."

Dad was the best computer fixer in the United States. Jen can remember that about him, but I can't.

"C'mon, Jen, you can fix it," I say to her.

Jen's tears are making her makeup run. I wonder if it's because she misses Dad or if it's because the computer is broken. I swipe them away with my sweatshirt sleeve.

Jen grins a fake grin and straightens up. Then she taps the side of the computer. It's a hard tap. More like a bang. *Wham!*

"It's coming on!" I yell. "You did it."

"Dad taught me that trick," Jen says proudly.

We find an icing recipe, and it doesn't take long to make at all. I sneak a lick off the spoon. It tastes like marshmallow cream. Jen shows me how to spread the icing ever so carefully. Without Jen, my cupcakes would be naked. I might not ever say this out loud to her, but I am glad she's my sister. At least today. She knows a lot about baking.

I make flowers on the tops of the cupcakes. I use raisins for the petals, celery for the stems, and lettuce for the leaves. Then I use sprinkles for the seeds in the middle. I'm thinking that I should probably label the flower parts. They don't look right without labels. But the cupcakes are small, and I don't have any room left.

We get the kitchen shined up. It's cleaner than before we started. Except for that blotchy spill in the oven. One of the cupcakes exploded.

Jen lights up the minute her phone goes *bling-a-ling*. It's a text message from Alien Timmy. She texts him back, then runs into her room. I should learn how to text so I can get a boyfriend, too. I would text message Todd first and ask:

Want 2 come 2 the mu c um?

If he said yes, I would text back, and make sure of one thing:

U R my BF now, right?

Worrying about boyfriends takes up lots of time, and the kitchen doesn't look like a party room yet. I get busy and blow up balloons until my lips are rubbery. Then I set the table with the fancy Christmas dishes. It doesn't seem fancy enough, so I dig out the Easter napkins. And add the Valentine's Day centerpiece that opens like a fan. I like being in the kitchen alone. I feel grown-up.

Mom walks in. She doesn't notice the balloons I've taped to the walls. Or the yummy smell. Or anything else! Balloons and cake fumes aren't such a big deal for a mom who celebrates birthdays for a living. I should have put up Halloween lights and black and orange streamers, too.

I step away from the table and yell, "Surprise! Happy birthday, Mom." I show her my cupcakes.

Jen charges in just in time to sing "Happy Birthday" with me.

Happy birthday to you.

Happy birthday to you.

Happy birthday, best mom in the world.

Happy birthday to you.

But Jen messes up the song because the wrong music comes out of her mouth. We sound like a toy that's running out of batteries. And when we get to the third line, Jen sings it wrong. She sings:

Happy birthday, dear old Mommm.

Mom isn't saying a word. Maybe she's not happy about the "dear old" part. Or maybe she's heard that birthday song too many times. Or seen one too many balloons in her forty years.

"What the matter?" I ask. I'm secretly shaking. And secretly hoping I am not in trouble. Mom's eyes are watery. Her nose is red. I probably shouldn't have cooked. Or baked. Or *whatever*.

I should have *made* a necklace out of ziti. A pasta necklace would have worked better than dumb old cupcakes.

Mom scoops up me and Jen in one big hug. It's hard to breathe. It's also hard to talk.

"But you're crying," I squeak. "Are you mad?"

"These are happy tears," Mom says.

I look over at Jen. Maybe she can explain to me what happy tears are. But Jen is sniffling and snuffling too. Sometimes I don't get this family.

"Thanks, girls," Mom says, wiping her nose. "What a surprise!"

Did she just say *girls?* But this was my idea. I'm the party planner. It's *my* birthday surprise, not Jen's!

"I planned the surprise, Mom. I made the cupcakes. By myself."

"You did not!" Jen says. "We both did."

"*What?* What did you do? Huh? Run the mixer? Google some icing? Search for the latest and greatest fall fashions on the internet? Text your alien boyfriend? Huh? Huh?"

I stomp my foot. I try to think of something else mean to say, but my brain can't come up with anything. Maybe it's because I have this counting going on in my head. One

. . . two . . . three . . . Or maybe it's because I'm not that mad at Jen.

Mom and Jen are staring at me. Like they know I'll say more. And I do. "Mom, Jen is right. We both did this. Together."

"Really?" Mom asks. "How nice! Sam, I've been quite hard on you lately. I've changed my mind about the Grand Canyon trip. Of course you can go."

I cannot believe my plan worked. And it worked before I got the chance to give Mom her rock collection present. Grand Canyon National Park, here comes Samantha Hansen!

All I have to do now is get ready for tonight's talent show. I'll need rocks, my special lamp, the old iPod that has music on it, a tablecloth, and one more thing from Jen. And I should practice what I'm going to say when I'm onstage. And what I'm going to do backstage. I hope I can get through the show without getting grounded.

12

A TALENT THAT SHINES

SINCE WE EACH ATE a teeny slice of birthday cupcake for dinner, we have a huge amount of tuna-broccoli casserole for dessert. Tuna-broccoli casserole tastes a whole lot better without the broccoli. And without the tuna, I'm sure.

Mom is taking me to the talent show. Jen isn't coming because she has a big test tomorrow. So she says. I wish Jen could be in the audience. She won't see how I'm planning to use her metal nail files for my talent. She won't see how I fix my "boy trouble" from yesterday.

"You put everything in the car, right, Mom?" I ask. "Especially the iPod?"

"Everything is in that blue bag, Sam. Are you going to sing?"

I shake my head.

"Dance?"

I shake my head. "It's a surprise," I say.

When we get to the school, I go to Mrs. Montemore's class. We have to wait in there until the show starts.

Kelli is tapping up and down the aisles between the desks. She's doing Irish step dancing for her talent.

"I can't use my hands. Only my feet," Kelli says, tapping left and right and in circles. "Sam, make sure my hands are not moving. They cannot fly up unless I do a clap like this." Kelli taps, stops, does a single clap, and then taps again. "And tell me if I smile. My dance teacher says I'm not supposed to smile. This is a serious Irish dance."

I can tell that serious dancing is hard for Kelli. She's a smiley kid.

Nick, the class clown, is practicing his jokes. I won't tell him, but none of his jokes are funny.

Todd is by himself in the corner doing air guitar to rock music. When he gets onstage, I bet his *ab-so*-lutely perfect teeth light up the place.

Richard walks in carrying his tuba. His talent is to play that weird-looking instrument blindfolded in the dark. When he explained this to us in class, that's when I came up with my plan to get back at That Kid.

"Line up," Mrs. Montemore calls.

We sit on the floor in front of the auditorium until it's time to go backstage. My stomach has butterflies that feel more like pterodactyls. In no time at all, Mrs. Montemore motions for me to follow her. It's my turn! The curtain is down when I walk onstage to get ready. I quickly cover my table with Mom's purple-checkered tablecloth. Then I put my special white and gray rocks on top in a perfect circle.

As the curtain goes up, I find *Star Wars* on the iPod and music booms out of the large speakers on the wall. I'm not sure why I picked *Star Wars*. I think it's because that music makes people pay attention.

I swing my arm over my rocks like I'm about to introduce them. And I am! "This is calcite – it's from England. This is fluorite—it's from China."

The audience oohs and aahs when I say "China."

"And this one is youngite. It's from wild Wyoming, and this last one—hydromagnesite—is from my backyard."

I had to practice how to say that last name. Over and over. Tonight it comes out exactly right, and I feel my stomach pterodactyls stop fluttering. I'm not worried one bit that nobody has clapped yet. I still haven't done the best part of my talent.

"These are my favorite gray, white, and tan rocks. Aren't they pretty?"

A few people cough. A little girl squirms out of her seat. Everybody else is rock-solid still—like the stalactites at Slippery Stone Cave.

I nod to Mrs. Montemore, who is standing by the side curtain. Then I reach under the table for my special lamp. Mrs. Montemore flips the auditorium light switch off, and I flip my lamp on. My lamp spreads ultraviolet light across the table and my rocks glow in the dark! That's because they're fluorescent rocks. The calcite is pinkish red. The fluorite is blue. The youngite is green. The hydromagnesite is purple.

A few kids whisper. Five, or maybe ten, grown-ups clap. Then everybody is quiet. *Ab-so*-lutely dead quiet. That's it? Were they expecting me to sing? Were they hoping I was going to Irish step dance around my rocks? I shuffle off the stage, pulling my rock table with me. Ling and Kristin are backstage.

"You bombed," Kristin says. "We could see your rocks from here, but the audience out there couldn't. You should have fixed your rocks at a forty-five-degree angle."

I have no idea why a forty-five-degree angle would make a difference. It must have something to do with the temperature on the stage. But how would making the room colder have helped me not bomb? Ling must know because she is jiggling her head like the bobble-head doll in Uncle Paul's car.

"It's our turn," Ling tells me. "We're performing a ballet. Our music is from *The Nutcracker*. Our talent will be so much better than yours."

I scoop up my biggest rock. I feel like plopping it on Ling's pink-ribboned slipper, but I'm more sad than mad.

I count anyway, "One, two, three, four." I turn and walk into the girls' bathroom. "Five, *ten*," I say a little louder. So I skipped a few. Nobody can hear me over that nutty music anyway.

I take out Jen's metal nail files and file off teeny bits of fluorite. It almost looks like gray dust, but soon it will be blue. I scoop the dust into a tissue and head backstage.

Richard is there doing lip exercises. He has to warm up that big mouth before he plays the tuba. As I pass by That Kid, I smile much too sweetly and sort of accidentally bump into him. I let the dust fall out of the tissue onto his head.

"Hey, watch it, freak," Richard says.

I pretend not to hear him, and I charge down the backstage steps to find a seat in the front row.

Pretty soon the curtain opens and Richard walks onstage. "I will take this blindfold and put it over my eyes," he says, barking like a circus seal. "I am in total darkness."

I bet he's cheating. It's a see-through blindfold, I'm sure.

"Lights out, please," he says to Mrs. Montemore.

This is the part I've been waiting for. Richard starts playing the "Star-Spangled Banner" on his tuba, and I aim my ultraviolet lamp toward his head.

And it works! Richard's red hair has bright blue dust in it. It sparkles and glows in the dark. Holy cannoli! He looks ridiculous. Like a clown. He won't call me names ever again.

The audience giggles. A few people ask if this is part of his act. Richard can't see why everybody is laughing, even when he takes off his blindfold.

"Richard, I like your blue hair!" shouts his sister, a kindergartener.

"Check out your reflection in your tuba," says a fifth-grader.

Richard looks. He rubs his hair and looks again. Then he darts off the stage.

I turn off my lamp, and the audience claps. A parent behind me says, "Wow, what a clever act! Didn't Richard's red hair look marvelous with that blue sprinkled in? And with the white curtain behind him, it made such a wonderful, patriotic display."

Now the clapping is getting louder and louder. And people start standing up. They love his act? Oh, no! This wasn't supposed to happen!

Richard comes out for a bow. He's not embarrassed like I

hoped he'd be. He's smiling. Then Richard stops smiling. He looks down at the front row. And straight at me!

A few minutes later, I see Richard making his way to the auditorium floor. He changes places with Arnie, so he can sit next to me. My stomach pterodactyls are doing full-speed soaring.

"You put the blue in my hair, didn't you?" Richard asks. "How'd you do it?"

I forget how to talk, so I pull out my ultraviolet lamp, my fluorite rock, and the tissue. The tissue still has specks of rock dust in it because when I bumped into Richard and sprinkled him, some got stuck. I hold out the tissue and Richard looks at it closely.

"Pretty amazing trick. Guess you're not so freakish after all."

Richard smiles at me so much that both his dimples show. I'm thinking that he doesn't look so tough anymore.

13

ON OUR WAY

MOM WAKES ME FRIDAY MORNING before Ren the rooster has a chance to cock-a-doodle. At first, I think it's a school morning, but then I remember. I'm skipping school today because we're catching a plane to Las Vegas! And then we're driving to the Grand Canyon! I will be standing in front of that canyon by the end of the day!

Uncle Paul picks us up at five o'clock. He's dropping us off at the Philadelphia airport. The drive seems like ten minutes.

That's probably because I fell asleep again without even trying.

Airports are busy places. People hurry in different directions, including us. I follow Mom left. Then right. Whoops! Wrong turn. Left again. We lose Jen for a minute, and move away from the people traffic until she catches up. Ladies in blue uniforms pull wheelie suitcases, men shout on cell phones and pull suitcases, and moms and dads yakkety-yak to each other and pull their kids.

Finally, we get to the place where we need to wait in line. It's not long, but it's moving slower than the slugs in my yard. Not a single person is hurrying here! My legs itch because of so much standing in one place.

"Mom, this is taking forever," I say. "Why do we need to wait in this line? We could have been there by now!"

A grouchy guard frowns at Mom. He coughs a big cough in my direction.

"Keep your voice down, Sam," Mom says. "This is the security line. All passengers must go through it. Be patient. And be quiet."

"But my left foot is asleep," I tell Mom. "And my right foot is the only thing propping me up, and . . ."

Jen turns to face the other direction. "I am *so* not listening to this," she says. She puts white buds in her ears and pretends she's not part of our family.

Mom shushes me again. I'm too excited to argue, plus the grouchy security guard now has on a don't-mess-with-me face. He reminds me of a scary robot I saw in a movie once. I grab Mom's hand.

Mom passes through the metal detector thing. Then it's my turn. A lady with thick goggle glasses points to Ace, my stuffed penguin, and then points to a moving belt. She wants me to put poor Ace in that machine? Can't she see he's my friend? Mom mouths, "It's OK," and I kiss Ace and lay him on the belt. If he gets shredded or eaten in there, I'm telling on that lady.

I go through the arch, then rescue Ace. Jen is next.

Beep. Beep. Beep.

The whole metal detector wakes up. Another lady takes Jen aside. Jen takes off her earbuds, earrings, and chain-link belt. And she walks through again.

Beep. Beep. Beep.

Off comes Jen's ankle bracelet and Alien Timmy's class ring.

BEEEEEEP.

This time the lady takes Jen out of line and fans a baseball bat wand up and down and over her. Then she whispers something in Jen's ear, and Jen is allowed back in line.

"Is everything all right, Jen?" Mom asks.

"It was just a dumb mistake, Mom. We better hurry. We don't want to miss our flight."

While Mom is busy moving through the people traffic, I ask Jen, "Why do you beep, and I don't?"

"Promise you won't tell?" Jen asks.

I shake my head, but I'll tell Mom. Someday. Jen knows this, I'm sure.

"I got my bellybutton pierced," Jen tells me.

"What?" I say to Jen with wide-open eyes. Holy cannoli! I have a huge secret. A just-between-sisters secret. This is going to be some trip!

We head down another long hallway, and halfway to our gate, the beeping starts again. Jen jumps out of her skin, and I giggle. It's just the shuttle trying to get by. I wave to somebody's grandma who's sitting on the shuttle. She shakes her cane at me.

After an hour, we're finally sitting on the plane. I have a window seat, Jen has the aisle, and Mom is in the middle. There are a lot of pretty great things to do on a plane—like pulling the mini window shade up and down, turning the overhead light on and off, and snapping the clips that hold the hidden tray in the seat in front of me. I want to unclip that tray, but when I reach for it, Mom whispers, "Don't touch."

The engines hum louder and louder, and we finally take off. "My ears feel like they're exploding," I shout.

"What's exploding?" Mom asks.

The heavy-duty military man in front of Mom zaps his head around to stare at us.

"Are your ears exploding, too?" I ask him.

Heavy-duty military man winks at me and turns to face the front again. I look out the window. The houses and roads get teeny and disappear. We fly straight through a wispy cloud. I wonder if it's the cirrus kind. It's like one big white streamer stretched across the sky. I *ab-so*-lutely like clouds a lot, and I have a cloud chart in my room. I can find out for sure what that streamy cloud is when I get home. And I'll learn about clouds when we get to the "Weather" chapter in our science book. Mrs. Montemore will be a great cloud teacher.

To take my mind off my exploding ears, I take out my notebook and write:

CLOUDS I SORT OF KNOW

1. Cirrus: pretty white clouds that look like hair that's been blown around by the wind
2. Cumulonimbus: dark, ghostly thunderclouds
3. Cumulus

I can't remember what a cumulus cloud is. But I remember its name because it sounds like cumulonimbus. But cumulonimbus is more fun to say. When I first saw cumulonimbus on my cloud chart, I had to practice that name. Over and over. It took me a week before I could say it right. It took me two weeks to learn how to say it without giggling.

We're nine-sixths of the way to Las Vegas when a pretty lady serves us sandwiches and juice. There isn't a piece of cake in sight! Only three peanut butter cookies. All for me! But this lunch smells awful. Like Parmesan cheese.

I feel someone's feet kick under my seat and the smell gets yuckier. I look under there and see that those feet aren't wearing any shoes. It's those stinky feet that are stinking up my lunch! Mom and Jen are snoozing, so I peek around to say something to the teenager behind me. "Hey, dude, it's against the rules to take off your shoes," I lie. I hope I sound older and more important than a ten-year-old. "Didn't you pay attention when the lady explained all that stuff in the beginning?"

Stinky-feet teen looks at me funny. He slides his feet back into his sneakers.

A man with very nice hair takes my trash and asks me if I'd like a pillow. When I say yes, he gives me a kid-size one. I wonder when he'll get Mom and Jen their regular-size pillows.

With Ace by my side, I snuggle against the wall.

Bump. Bumpitybumpbump. BUMP.

Our plane is landing? We're in Las Vegas? Time has played a trick on me again. It jumps like magic when I'm sound asleep. We pick up our carry-on stuff and get ready to leave. Mom says, "After we get our luggage, we'll get in the rental car and start our road trip."

"Oh, hooray!" I shout. I hope the pilot walking down the aisle doesn't yell at me. Wait. What's he doing back here with the passengers? Who drove the plane?

When we get to the luggage pick-up place, we watch for our bags to ride down the ramp and onto the luggage merry-go-round. I'm thinking that it would be fun to be luggage. Round and round I'd go.

We stand in two more lines, but these lines move fast. I bet everybody at the airport wants to get to the Grand Canyon! Just like us.

Before long, I'm sitting in the back of the car. Jen sits next to Mom because Mom says she needs her to "navigate." Navigators navigate better in the ocean, I think, but I'm keeping this thought to myself.

Jen opens the map app on her phone. I peek over her shoulder and see the colorful lines that show us the way to the canyon. The map lady starts to talk, and I ask Jen how long the drive is. She ignores me, so I ask Mom, "How long will this take? We better hurry. It's noon already."

"I figure it will take us five hours, Sam. Get comfortable. Enjoy the scenery. It doesn't look anything like Pennsylvania, does it?"

Mom is right. It's a desert out here. I've never seen so much flatness. Where are all the trees? And the grassy lawns? I see dozens of big, fancy hotels from the highway. One has a weird cat statue parked outside. That same cat is in an Egypt book I checked out of the library. It's called a Shrinks or Sinx or something.

"Hey, that cat should be in Egypt," I tell Mom. "Who moved it?"

"It hasn't been moved, Sam," Mom says. "That's the city of Las Vegas, Nevada. Keep your eyes peeled. In no time at all, we'll be at the Hoover Dam."

"Are you serious? Do we need a dam stop?" I look at Mom's reflection in the rearview mirror and wonder if she's going to holler at me for saying a word that sounds like a swear word. "Will we get to the Grand Canyon before dark? How can I see the Grand Canyon at night? C'mon, Mom. You told me . . ."

Instead of Mom driving faster, she is slowing down. Is she going to pull over and make me settle down? That will take up too much time. Before she has the chance to move the car off the road, I count. Out loud. "One, two, three, four . . . What I mean to say is . . . Will we *please* get a chance to *maybe* see the Grand Canyon before dark?"

Mom shakes her head. And I can tell from her head-shaking that I should shut up. Big time. Jen shakes her head, too. Why can't she mind her own business? My foot sneaks around between Jen's seat and the side door. It bumps into her right elbow—the elbow that has a scab on it from where she fell at track practice.

"*Ow-wah!*" Jen yells. "What are you doing? Put your feet on your mat. Like, now!"

"I was stretching," I tell her. "Trust me. I don't want to get in any trouble."

Jen opens her mouth to complain, but instead she just sighs.

"Oh, *puh-leeze.*" She picks up her cell phone and starts texting everybody on the planet.

I scoot to the front edge of my seat, as far as my seatbelt will let me. Jen's texting at the speed of light. I knew that long speed-of-light number once, but now I forget.

"Stop spying on me," Jen says.

"Wanna teach me to do that?" I ask in my lovable-little-sister voice—the same sweet voice I used when I asked Jen to help me with Mom's cupcakes.

"What? Text your friends?" she asks.

"I bet I can do it," I tell her. I type an imaginary message into my imaginary cell phone. "Look, my thumbs are in super shape."

Jen flips her hair. And she does something I cannot believe. She hands me her cool-looking phone!

"Do any of your friends have cell phones?" she asks.

"No," I say. "Can I text one of yours?"

Jen is about to say no, I think. But she doesn't! She points to a spot on the screen, and says, "Press that. You'll get to my contacts."

It's hard to do. That spot is smaller than my pinky fingernail. I keep making the screen change. How does Jen do this? She makes it look so easy. When I do get to her contacts, I stare at the first name that pops up on her list: Chrissy. My insides get wiggly, like the gelatin Mom puts in her Bungee-Jump Cake. Chrissy is Todd's big sister!

"Chrissy," I spit out. "I want to text Chrissy. Her brother is in my class."

"Ooh, I get it," Jen says.

I'm not sure if Jen's "Ooh" means she knows I like Todd, or what, but she's letting me use her phone, so I don't care.

I want to type: *This is Samantha Hansen. Tell Todd I say hi!* in the little box. But my message comes out: *Thisisss Sammm Hansnn. Telll Toddd hi.*

Jen says I hold my thumbs on the letters too long. And she isn't mean about it at all. She shows me how to send my message. Off it goes!

"Wow, thanks," I say. I hand her the phone and give her arm a quick, lovable pat. I'm very careful not to touch her left elbow. That one might have a scab, too.

Then I turn to look at the scenery. There's not much new to see. I wonder how my message flies across that scenery and through the air to get to Chrissy. And I wonder if Chrissy will give that message to Todd. A yawn slides out, and to keep myself awake, I think about a new list:

WHY I HOPE MY MESSAGE GETS TO TODD

1. Todd has eyes like coal. Or obsidian, a prettier, glassier, black rock I just learned about.
2. Todd has ab-so-lutely perfect teeth.
3. Todd likes rocks and caves.
4. Todd plays air guitar.
5. Todd is nothing like That Kid Richard.

14

HOOVER DAM JAM

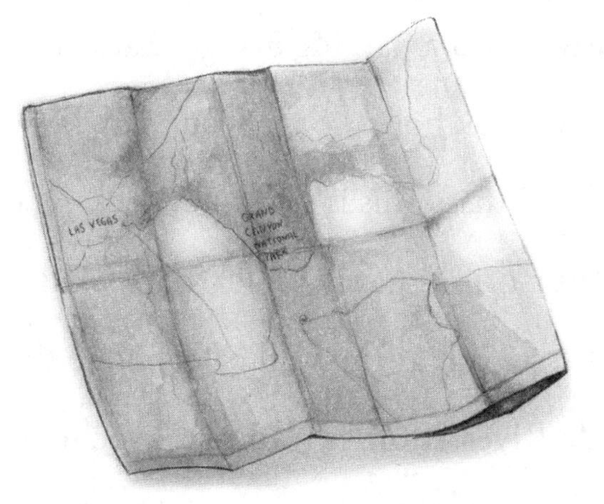

WE ARE TRAVELING UP a steep hill at the Hoover Dam place. And we're stuck in a long line of cars, trucks, and vans. This line makes me itchy. Like I was at the airport, only it's my butt that's asleep instead of my foot.

I tap Mom's shoulder. "After this trip, I am not waiting in any more lines. For the rest of my life."

Mom laughs. "Relax, Sam. We're pulling over in a minute to get a breath of fresh air, stretch our legs, and get something to drink. You girls should see this dam since we're here. It's an amazing piece of engineering."

Jen moans.

I moan, too.

For once, we both agree. Seeing a dam isn't a great idea.

Mom drives into a parking garage that's cut out of golden rock. I want to look bored so we won't stay long, but I have a hard time doing that. This is one fancy rock garage!

We get our drinks at the snack bar. While I chug-a-lug my water, I stare out at the wall of concrete that holds back the Colorado River. Mom is reading a brochure that explains how it was built. I don't care about that. Neither does Jen. We complain enough so that Mom can't stand to hear us anymore, and she tells us it's time to get back on the road. I'm glad to see there is not one bit of traffic as we leave that dam place.

"Hey, Mom, can I call Kelli?"

Mom hands me her phone. It's easy typing in Kelli's home number. My fingers are warmed up from texting.

"Hi, Kelli, it's me, Sam."

"Sam, hi!" Kelli shouts. "I've been dying to talk to you! Everybody—I mean the whole school—is going on and on about you."

"Oh, no. Am I in trouble with Principal Tancredi again?" I ask Kelli in a hushed voice. "That lady is out to get me. Do you think I'll be kicked out of school? This is about the talent show, isn't it?" I'm talking really fast, like Mom does when she's had two pots of coffee.

"*Noooo*, Principal Tancredi wasn't at the talent show," Kelli tells me. "It's not that. It's what you did to Richard Frey's hair. That light show you put on top of his head. It was terrific. My mom snapped a shot of him with her phone. Richard looked like a glow-in-the dark, tuba-playing dork."

"I wanted to get back at him for being mean to me, Kell. I wanted him to be embarrassed. But my plan backfired. He thought it was a cool joke."

"I know. I know," Kelli says. "Wait till you hear this. Richard thinks you're awesome now. He *really* likes you. He told me at recess when you weren't there today."

"*What?*" I yell.

"Sam, not so loud," Mom says. "I'm trying to concentrate on my driving."

"Richard doesn't like me," I whisper. "Not one bit. But wait. Last night, when he came off the stage, he purposely wanted to sit next to me. He said I wasn't freakish, or something. I didn't pay attention. Much. But I did think it was strange that he was nice to me. And he smiled. A lot. Did you know that Richard has dimples? I never noticed those dimples before."

"His dimples were showing all over the place when he talked about you today. He's going to call you when you get home. And guess what? You are not gonna believe this. He wants you to go out for ice cream with him."

My head is spinning. I want Todd to be my boyfriend. Not Richard. I think.

"But Kell, I like Todd. You heard him stick up for me at the cave. He is much nicer than Richard."

Kelli babbles on some more. "Yes, but Todd is shy. Shy boys are *bor*-ing. That's just how it is. Plus, I heard a rumor that Todd is moving. He probably won't be coming to our school for much longer."

This is terrible news. I'm more miserable now than I was at the dam. I say good-bye to Kelli, give Mom her phone, and slump into my seat. Now which boy should I like—the boy who likes me, or the boy who's moving far, far away?

We drive for twenty minutes, then I hear Mom say, "Uh, oh."

There is no time for an "uh-oh" on this trip, I'm sure.

"What's the matter, Mom?" Jen asks.

"I think I took a wrong turn at the Hoover Dam," Mom answers. "Was I supposed to get back in that line of traffic and drive *over* the dam? Over the Colorado River? Hmm. Jen, did I miss a turn?"

Jen shrugs, looks at the map on her phone, and tries to figure out where Mom got mixed up.

"Just forget it," Mom says. "I need a real map—a *paper* map that has Nevada and Arizona on it. The car rental place gave us one. Jen, check that envelope that has the rental contract. I think there's one in there."

Jen finds the map and Mom pulls over to study it. I look out the back window. The line to the dam is now four times longer than it was before!

"Well, we'll just take a detour to the south here," Mom says, folding the map in half. She sounds like she knows where she's going, I think. The next time I do this trip, I'm taking a train from the Philly station to the Grand Canyon station.

Our "detour" is two hours long. We actually drive through a teeny piece of eastern California—maybe twenty-sixteenths of it. California is not near the Grand Canyon. I may only be in the fourth grade, but even a fourth-grader knows that much! I mention this to Mom.

"I'm on the right road now, Sam," Mom says. "Don't worry. We'll get there."

At first, I didn't mind staring at the pretty mountains, but now I'm sick of them. Outside there is nothing but green, green, green. Evergreen trees are everywhere. The Grand Canyon is a beautiful red, brown, tan, and gray with a *little* green. I bet we're not ten-thirds of the way to Arizona yet. Mom probably made another wrong turn at that fake Hoover Dam we went over. I am so sleepy—sleepier than I was when I stayed up till two a.m. at Kelli's birthday sleepover. But I'm staying awake if it kills me.

Hours and hours pass before Mom stops the car and says, "We're here. Well, not at the canyon, of course. It's about a mile up the road. We'll stay at this motel tonight and rest. Let's get unpacked and get to bed. We have a big day tomorrow."

What? I must be dreaming a nightmare. We are parked under a sign that says:

BARELY INN

JUST A SNORE AWAY FROM THE GRAND CANYON

The words are carved out of wood. We drive miles and miles and miles to check into a motel and sleep? How can anybody sleep at a time like this? And how can the grandest canyon on Earth be stuck in the middle of a forest?

"Mom, if the Grand Canyon is near here, I have to see it. Now! I've waited my whole life . . ."

"Ugh," Jen says. "I am *so* not going to listen to this. I'm outta here. I wonder if there's a hot tub in this place."

"Sam, let's go," Mom says.

I am not budging. "I don't want to. I want to see the canyon. *Now*. I want to—"

Mom cuts me off. "Count, Sam. Right this minute. Because if you don't, I will turn this car right around, and we'll go home."

I crawl toward the door and shout, "One." And let out a loud sigh. *Pshoo!* "Two." I probably wake the deer that live in this piney forest. "Three, four, five, six." I feel another sigh coming on, but it weirdly turns into a yawn. Counting is too much work tonight. It's easier to cooperate, I'm sure.

When I step outside, I notice how different it is here. There are no cars on the road, no traffic lights or neon signs. No farms, barns, or cornstalks. It's quiet except for some owls hooting to each other. The air smells crispy and clean like freshly washed clothes. I take a deep breath and smell smoke from a fireplace. It reminds me of the toast Mom makes me for a bedtime snack. It reminds me how far away from home I am.

In the motel room, I unpack and think about tomorrow. We're going to see the canyon's south side, called the South Rim. And we're hiking down Bright Angel Trail to the bottom and staying overnight in a tent! I want to ride a burro instead, but

Mom says it'll be more of an adventure this way. What she really means is that hiking is cheaper than burro riding.

I'm not sure how far down the bottom is. The only place my feet ever hiked before was in my backyard. And the steps I hiked up to Slippery Stone Cave. I'm thinking that hiking to the bottom of the Grand Canyon is much farther than that. I want to ask Mom exactly how far it is, but she's sound asleep already.

"Hey, Jen?"

"Go to sleep," Jen says. "You're sharing a bed with Mom. Not me."

"At least Mom won't snore in my ear," I tell her. And using my lovable-little-sister voice, I ask, "Will you do my hair in a spiky cinnamon bun in the morning? It's a very important day for me."

"Sure, Sam," Jen whispers. "But you're on your own if a mother eagle decides to make a nest out of it."

Jen is kidding.

I think.

15

BARELY INN

I WAKE AT SEVEN O'CLOCK the next morning because an invisible alarm clock has gone off in my head. I jump into my new hiking outfit and boots and march around the room.

Clomp. Clomp. Clomp.

Jen and Mom have no choice but to wake up. The bus that takes us to the South Rim comes to Barely Inn at nine o'clock. Mom needs at least four cups of coffee. She doesn't talk in complete sentences until her third cup. And Jen needs an hour to curl her hair. I'm thinking I'll have Jen do the spiky bun thing another day. Today I'm not in the mood for being a bird's nest. Especially with eagles flying around.

Mom and Jen aren't getting out of bed fast enough. I don't want to be late, so I add some loud singing to my stomping:

Happy Grand Canyon to us.

Happy Grand Canyon to us.

If we don't get movin' soo-oon,

We'll all miss the bus.

While Mom and Jen are getting ready, I head to the lobby. There is a rack in the corner with a hundred brochures. There are colorful brochures about rafting, canoeing, camping, horseback riding, helicopter rides, mountain climbing—tons of Grand Canyon activities. There's a small brochure about the Hula-pie-whatever Reservation. I'm pretty sure that's where Native Americans live. I ask the lady at the front desk about them.

"The Hualapai Tribe own a million acres of the Grand Canyon, sweetie," the Barely Inn lady says. "They are very much a part of the community, and they often entertain our tourists with their traditional dances. If you get a chance to see the show, you'll learn about their culture as well."

The Barely Inn lady reminds me of the chatty car salespeople on TV. I should tell her I'm not here to learn about culture. Instead I say, "I just want to see the most *ab-so*-lutely beautiful sedimentary rocks on Earth."

The Barely Inn lady winds herself up to talk again. "Well, then, you will certainly want to venture out on the Skywalk. I haven't had the chance to go out on this horseshoe-shaped deck, but I hear it is simply fantastic. It's one-of-a-kind, you know. It extends seventy feet from the canyon rim, four thousand feet above the canyon floor. Let's see, I believe I have some brochures on it. And did you know, the Hualapai had to give the investors permission to build it on their land? How lovely of them to allow this. Oh, here they are. Give these to your mom or dad, OK? They won't want to miss such a fabulous opportunity."

I recognize that glass horseshoe. "Thanks!" I say with pretend excitement. "I'll take them all!" If I take every single one, then Mom won't see this thing. She won't make this part of our "adventure."

By the time I skip down the hallway to our room, the Skywalk brochures have found a home in an empty trashcan. In the room, I'm happy to see that Mom and Jen are dressed. Mom looks relaxed and ready to go in her tan hiking shorts, T-shirt, and very huge backpack. Jen looks like she needs to be in a magazine with a headline that says, "Hiking Don'ts."

"You mean I have to carry my sleeping bag on my back?" she whines. "What will that do to my posture?"

"Jen, if your sister can do it, so can you," Mom tells her. And she winks at me.

Nobody told me I had to carry my bed on my back. I don't want Jen to see I have a lot of questions about this, too, so I keep my mouth shut.

Less than fifteen minutes later, we're out the door.

During that never-ending mile ride to the canyon, I keep my nose glued to the bus window. All I see is green—just like the night before. I'm a little worried that the Grand Canyon isn't as great-looking in person as it is in a book.

The bus stops and we pile out. Jen takes a minute to adjust her hair. Mom gulps the last few drops of her coffee.

I notice an arrow on a sign that has a picture of a lookout platform. I've seen that platform in my book. I know the canyon is just ahead. I take off through the parking lot and up the hill. I'm running faster than a cheetah, I'm sure.

Before I get to the platform, I spy the Grand Canyon. It's pretty hard to miss! I blink my eyes because I cannot believe that what I'm seeing is real. The canyon is *huge!* More huge than anything I've ever seen—more huge than the Tri-County Mall! It goes on and on for miles. There are cliffs and plateaus, and more and more cliffs and plateaus as far as I can see. Seeing this much rock in one place is quite possibly the best thing ever.

The rock layers sit on top of each other like Mom's layered cakes. But here, each layer is a different kind of rock. The colors—black, red, brown, tan, yellow, white—bounce off my eyeballs. I cannot believe I am *not* looking at a picture. I blink and blink again. The picture is still there!

Ever so carefully, I look down. I can almost see the bottom! Saber-toothed tigers and other animals hung out there millions of years ago. Maybe I'll find a rare mammoth fossil and it'll be put in a museum and named after me: The Samantha Hansen Mammoth, or the Sam Mam for short.

I open my notebook and on the very top, I write:

STUFF TO DO

1. Take a fossil from the Grand Canyon.

But there are signs everywhere that say not to take anything—not even a teeny rock or a lump of clay or mud. So I cross out "take" and put in a better word.

1. ~~Take~~ Borrow a fossil from the Grand Canyon.

If a ranger asks me, I'll tell him I'm planning to give it back to the canyon the next time I visit here. Next year. When I come by train.

Jen sneaks up behind me and tickles my ribs. "Gotcha," she says.

My pencil flies into the canyon. I don't hear it land.

I zip around and almost yell at her for scaring me. I guess maybe I thought I would fall into the canyon, but that would be hard to do. It's hard to fall through a closed-in railing that's taller than you.

"Jen, quit fooling around," I say. "I'm looking at one of the Seven Wonders of the Natural World, you know."

"That *is* some serious rock out there," Jen says. "I've got to admit it, Sam, this place is pretty darn cool. I've never seen anything like it. You're glad we're finally here, huh?"

"*Ab-so*-lutely." I nod and stare out at the canyon.

Jen nods and stares, too.

Other people step on and off the platform, but I never let my eyes leave the scenery in front of me. I still cannot believe I'm not dreaming. With my binoculars, I see hundreds of valleys, plateaus, and mountains up close. The Grand Canyon stretches on forever, I'm sure.

Mom walks over to us. She introduces me and Jen to Chad, our hiking guide. Jen's eyes get googly-woogly. I hear her mumble, "Geez, he's cute," under her breath.

I can't help but make a kissy face in her direction, just to get back at her for tickling me.

"Good morning," Chad says. "Are you ready to hike Bright Angel Trail?"

Jen says good morning the loudest. She nudges her way to the front of the group.

Chad starts his tour-guide talk. "Welcome to the South Rim," he says, swooping his arms out in front of him. "We'll start our hike on a trail that runs west to east. Just past that building over there is the entrance to Bright Angel. As you can probably see, there are no railings on these trails. Be very careful."

Chad smiles and waves for us to come closer.

Jen wants to look important, so she waves with him. "Let's get moving, people," she says with her bossy-big-sister voice—the one she uses to annoy me.

I get in line behind Jen, but I only pay attention to Chad. "Do not leave the trail at any time," he says. "Watch each step. Be careful and don't rush. Stay together. We don't want to lose any hikers on this trip."

I wonder how Chad can be so calm. Didn't he read that book in the souvenir store about all those people who got lost here?

As we leave the platform and start to walk along the edge of the canyon, Chad says, "Once we head onto Bright Angel, it's a bit more than nine miles to the bottom. Is everybody ready for an exhilarating day?"

Jen starts to moan, but then she makes it sound more like a cough.

I turn to Mom with a wide-open mouth. Holy cannoli! Did Chad say nine *miles?*

16

IT'S A HIKE, ALRIGHT

BRIGHT ANGEL TRAIL is only as wide as two of my beds put together. It's scarier than I thought it would be, and I don't go within two feet of that million-foot drop-off.

My feet are barely moving, but my eyeballs are going left and right a mile a minute. I walk and walk and walk some more until I get brave enough to peek over the edge. It makes me dizzy, so I won't be doing that again.

I turn toward the canyon wall and press against it for a few seconds. And I see something. It's small, but it's there. Is it a fossil? Yep. I see a head and legs and an abdomen. I can imagine how it looked years and years ago. This bug fossil is the coolest thing *ever!*

"What's that?" Mom asks.

"A fossil," I say, rubbing my fingers along the wall. "Isn't it beautiful?"

Mom puts on her bifocals for a better look. "Wow, leave it to my scientist daughter to discover something so small in a place so big."

Mom and I walk along, touching the canyon walls and searching for more fossils. I find one that looks like a fish. Mom finds one that reminds her of a birthday cake, of course. I get tired of standing, so I stoop down for a minute. And right next to my hiking boot is a teeny rock with a fat fossil in it. Just like the one on the wall! I sneak that fossil into the pocket of my jacket.

The other hikers catch up to us and stop to look at what we're looking at. The riders on the burros jump off to see what's going on, too. When a burro stops near me, I finally understand why Kelli says they are stinky.

We start to hike again, and at every turn there is something new to see—like a ripply rock that has a hundred colors. I think it's a lava flow. Or a grayish peak that has a cloud stuck on it. Or the yellowish rock that has an evergreen tree growing out of it sideways.

Two miles click by. Chad motions for us to stop. "Let's rest for a few minutes and wait for that woman back there to catch up," he says. "I'll fill you in on some interesting canyon facts."

I cannot put a lid on my excitement. It's a good thing it's quiet here. I don't want to miss a single word Chad says. He probably went to park ranger school for twenty-fifths of his life to learn everything about the canyon.

"See that river down there?" Chad asks.

Jen makes sure Chad hears her answer. "Oh, I do! It's that beautiful line of dark blue." Jen flips her sunglasses on top of her head like a fashion model. "Ooh, look! It's the same color as my eyes."

My sister will do anything for attention. But it doesn't work. Chad ignores her. "Can anybody tell me about that river?"

"It's the Colorado River," I say. "It's one hundred feet deep in some places, and eighteen miles wide in some places. It's like a snake that weaves through the canyon. But the river doesn't start here. It starts high in the Rocky Mountains."

Chad looks at me and asks, "Hey, you're the one who found the fossils in the canyon walls, aren't you? You seem to know quite a lot about the Grand Canyon. What's your name?"

"Samantha Hansen."

Jen pokes me in the ribs, so I introduce her. "And this is my sister, Jennifer. We're here with our mom." I point to the only hiker who hadn't joined the group—the one who needed extra catching-up time.

"Well, Samantha Hansen—"

"You can call her Sam," Jen butts in. "And I'm Jen, of course. My friends call me Jen, not Jennifer." Jen smiles at Chad, then turns and crosses her eyes at me. I figured out a long time ago that this is Jen's way of reminding me she's almost a grown-up and I'm not even close.

"Jen and Sam, and everybody else," Chad says, "this entire canyon has been formed by erosion. Erosion is the process of wearing rock away. The Colorado River carried sand, mud, and rock with it over many, many years. The river carved these canyon walls."

"And the river *still* cuts through the rock," I can't help but say.

Chad nods. "Hey, Sam. Come on up front with me. I can use your help today. You can be my assistant."

I wiggle carefully past Jen. Her jaw drops so that her mouth looks like a big O. I want a mama bird to fly in there and make a nest on her tonsils.

When I'm next to Chad, I stand up really straight, like Mrs. Montemore does when she gives a lesson. This is the most important day of my life.

Chad puts his hand on my shoulder. "Sam, tell us what you find most fascinating about the Grand Canyon."

I take a deep breath, but no words come out. For a second, this day reminds me of the day at Slippery Stone Cave when Richard Frey made fun of me. I do a double-take just to make sure That Kid hasn't suddenly appeared out of nowhere.

"The Grand Canyon is one of the Natural Wonders of the World," I tell the hikers. "There are many types of rocks in the canyon. Wait. Let me get out my notes."

I dig in my backpack. When I find my notebook, I flip to the page where I wrote: "How Rocks Are Classified." I hold it up high, so all the hikers can see, and I read it.

HOW ROCKS ARE CLASSIFIED

1. Sedimentary Rocks: rocks from teeny bits of other rock and teeny organisms that get piled up VERY close to each other. They end up stuck together.

2. Igneous Rocks: rocks that start out as hot, gooey lava, but now they're cold. And hard—hard as rock!

3. Metamorphic Rocks: rocks that get a lot of pressure or heat. They get squished and folded, and changed. Every atom in them.

"Oh, *puh-leeze*," Jen chimes in.

"Yes, please, go on," Chad says. He gives Jen a teachery look.

Jen tosses her hair and acts like she doesn't care.

"The canyon has all three kinds of rock. The different layers of these rocks tell scientists—geologists, mostly—how old the canyon is." It's easy for me to talk about the canyon because I *ab-so*-lutely love this place. I want to live here when I'm grown up. I wonder if the park rangers will let me build a house on that very tall plateau in the middle."

I point to the very top where we started the trail. "The youngest rocks are up there," I say. Everybody looks. Everybody but Chad. Chad is smiling at me. So is Mom. Jen probably wants to smile at me, but her smile leans more toward Chad.

We hike and hike some more. We take a break at the Three-Mile Resthouse, but I'm too excited to rest. When we start walking again, Chad asks me if I can "continue to educate the group" about the Grand Canyon. He says he's enjoying being a listener instead of a talker today.

Jen thinks this is the funniest thing anybody has ever said.

She giggles for the next five minutes.

Mom shuts her up by saying, "Sam, can you speak a little louder? Some of us back here are having trouble hearing you over Jen. And you are such a terrific assistant tour guide."

Jen does her eye-roll thing.

"Jen, what do you know, huh? How to be a professional text messenger? Your phone doesn't get service down here, does it? How are you gonna text Alien Timmy? Huh? Huh?"

"Sam, that lid still has to stay on your temper. Count," Mom says. "Count *now*—before you scare the wildlife."

"One, two, three, four . . . five . . . six … seven. Eight. Nine. Ten." I am getting better and better at this. Besides, the thought of scaring wildlife scares *me*.

I hike fast and hope the group keeps up. I ask everybody if they know how some of the rock layers got crooked. No one guesses it's because of earthquakes, volcanoes, and bad weather. Maybe they don't guess because they're busy wishing for a ride from the burros that squeeze by.

Soon I run out of things to say. Plus, my throat feels like it got sprinkled with dirt. And my boots feel like they're full of dirt, too. Ten-ninths full, I think. I drop out of the front of the line and end up where Mom is, at the back.

"I know you're tired, Sam, but hang in there," Mom says.

Mom looks tired, too. More tired than me, and *way* more tired than the whistling eighty-year-old man in the baseball hat.

"We'll be at the bottom in twenty minutes," Chad calls.

Chad is wrong. It takes us an hour. Jen has to stop every five minutes because her feet are "falling off."

We make it all the way down. It wasn't easy. What a long day!

"I'll be back in fifteen minutes," Chad tells the group. "I'm heading over to the ranger station to check in. I know you're exhausted, so hang out here, rest, and drink plenty of water," he says. "When I return, I'll take you to your campsites, and we'll bunk down for the night."

I plop down and look up at that very tall canyon. My feet are worn out from hiking so many miles. My eyes are worn out from seeing so many beautiful rocks. I watch the sun drop down behind the canyon walls. As it does, the rays touch the rocks, and I see *way* more than black, red, brown, tan, yellow, and white. I see every color of the rainbow.

Mom comes to sit next to me. It feels good to have her to myself.

"Sam, I'm proud of how you've handled things on this trip. Especially with your sister. Have you seen Jen?" she asks.

"She's walking around trying to get a signal for her phone," I answer. "I saw her take off as soon as Chad did."

Mom's smile stops working. She stands up and looks for Jen. "Now why would she do that? Where would she go? Jen? Jen!"

"Maybe she's looking for Chad," I tell Mom.

Mom thinks about this for a minute, and then she starts pacing back and forth. "Jen! Jen-ni-fer!" she shouts in three separate syllables. "Where are you?"

There is no answer. Mom calls ten times. And ten times there is no answer. "Oh, Sam. I think Jen is lost!"

17

LOST OR FOUND?

CHILLS GO THROUGH ME when Mom says "lost." I remember what Kelli told me about the Grand Canyon: You don't want to get lost in that place. They'll never find you. My sister is a pain in the butt, but I don't want her lost forever.

"Sam!"

Mom's voice makes me jump.

"Did you hear that?" she asks me. "Sounds like thunder."

It does sound like thunder. I would know this for sure if

I saw a cumulonimbus cloud hanging around. But it's already too dark to see if any of those kinds of clouds are above us. A minute later, lightning shoots across the sky and more thunder comes.

Boom . . . Boom . . . Boom.

Now I know there are cumulonimbus clouds above us. I'm not afraid of storms when I'm inside. But this storm is big-time scary because the thunder gets stuck in the canyon and echoes off the canyon walls.

BoomBoomBoom!

It seems like the storm is inside my head.

"Sam, we have to find Jen," Mom says with a shaky voice. "Now! Let's go."

Mom grabs my hand and pulls me into the woods. The thunder booms change to sharp-sounding cracks that seem to go on forever.

CRA-A-A-CK!

More lightning lights up the sky. The zigzags go out in many directions like a spiderweb. It is *not* a good idea to be out here, I'm sure. We don't have a hiking guide. We aren't supposed to go anywhere without Chad. And I left every one of my trail maps back at the Barely Inn.

"Mom, Chad will know how to find Jen when he comes back. Shouldn't we wait?"

But Mom yanks me along, and we go deeper into the woods. It starts to rain. Hard. The little trail we are following is gone. It has blended into the rest of the brown mud. A picture of a skeleton flashes before my eyes. I hope Kelli is wrong about missing hikers turning into skeletons.

I flash my flashlight up ahead. "Mom, we passed this bunch of rocks before. We went in a circle."

"Oh, Sam, you're right. I'm a mess. I'm so worried about your sister. The storm is getting worse and worse."

"She's OK, Mom," I say, but I wonder if this is true.

Mom wrings her fingers like a kitchen dishrag. "We shouldn't be out here. I should have left you with the other hikers. They're safe and sound and dry now in the rest station. Now I've put us both in danger."

"But Mom," I say. "I think the storm is slowing down. Listen." Mom acts like she doesn't hear me. She just gets louder and louder.

"We needed this vacation. I wanted this vacation! But I shouldn't have brought you and Jen here. I … I thought I could do this. But apparently *not!* What was I thinking? I've never taken you and Jen anywhere alone . . . without your dad. He should be here with us! We need him."

"*Mom!*" I holler. "Count. Count to ten! Count with me!" I have to scream this so Mom hears me over her voice and the storm. I take both her hands, look into her teary eyes, and start. "One, two, three . . ."

Mom looks at me funny. Like she can see right through me. She doesn't say a word until I'm on number four. Then she joins me and together we make it to ten. Mom takes a deep breath—in and out—and so do I. We hug each other and breathe—in and out. And in and out some more.

"The storm is far away now," I say. "But in case it comes back I think I know of a place we can hide out for a while. At least until it stops raining hard. There's a teeny cave back there. To the left of that last turn."

Mom nods and lets me take her to the cave. We huddle inside and listen to the rain for a while without saying a word.

"This is a really nice cave," I say because I don't know what to say.

"Sam," Mom says. "I'm sorry. I lost it."

"Yep, I know. It happens to me all the time."

Mom tilts my chin up. I see her I-love-you face. "You are an amazing little girl. And you're a lot like your dad."

"I am?" I think about this for a full minute, before I start to talk. "I know Dad got sick, but you've never told me much else. Every time you start to say something about him, the color leaves your face. So I don't ask you anything."

Mom sniffles and blows her nose. "What do you want to know, Sam?"

"I want to know what his bad sickness was. I want to know how I'm like him. I want to know what part of me looks like him. I want . . . I want a picture of him for my room." My face is wet, but not from the rain.

Mom dabs my tears but stays quiet. The storm is quiet now, too. Little by little Mom tells me what I want to know—how Dad died of cancer, and that it happened so fast he didn't suffer. How he loved to figure out the way things worked—everything from computers to how to get the grass to grow. How he wished he had been a farmer because he loved the earth. Just like I love the earth.

"I don't want to be a farmer," I tell Mom.

"I know," Mom says. "But you love everything about the earth—the rocks, the weather, the bugs—even the dinosaurs that lived here many years ago."

"I guess so," I say.

"And there is a very special part of you that reminds me of Dad every day," Mom says in a soft voice.

"There is?"

"Well, it's something I wish I'd see more often, but it never shows up when you're losing your temper. It's your smile."

I smile and use my fingers to trace my lips.

"When you're happy," Mom says, taking my hand and kissing it, "it's like a part of Dad is still here."

"Hey, is somebody in there?" a familiar voice calls from the cave's opening.

It's Chad.

We crawl out and what do we see? Chad isn't the only one there. Jen is next to him. And she's not a skeleton! The first thing Mom does is hug Jen, of course. And Chad, too, but I don't know why.

"Where were you?" Mom hollers at Jen. "Sam saw you go off by yourself. We couldn't find you anywhere. You are fifteen years old, Jennifer Hansen, not twenty-five. If you ever do a stupid thing like that again, young lady, I'll . . ."

I don't pay much attention to what Mom is saying because I'm thinking of two things: I have my dad's smile. And I'm not getting into trouble. Jen is. Finally.

Jen scrunches her shoulders and explains, "When I couldn't get anybody on my phone, I got bored. I followed Chad, but then the storm started, and I didn't know where I was. Or how to get back to you. I wasn't lost for long before Chad came by and rescued me." Jen tosses her flippy hair in Chad's direction.

"Jen's fine, Mrs. Hansen," Chad says. "I found her walking around in the woods, so I took her with me to the ranger station.

She was pretty shaken. We stayed there until the storm passed. But what are *you* doing out here with Sam?" Chad asks. "How did the two of you find this cave?"

"Well," Mom says, "we foolishly went in search of Jen. It sure is easy to get lost out here. The storm washed out the trail. We wandered around in a circle, but as you know, Sam is quite the scientific observer. Not a whole lot gets by her. She noticed this cave, and we decided to wait in here."

"There's a bunch of caves in the Grand Canyon," I chime in. "That's because of the limestone." I mention a few other cave facts. I remember them from my trip to Slippery Rock Cave. Mom and Chad smile at me. Jen squeezes water from her jacket and smiles, too.

That night we sleep in a tent. A tent is a pretty great place. But I'm having trouble getting settled in. I miss my soft bed and my stuffed-animal friends. I snuggle closer to Ace, and he makes me feel better. He smells like home. I turn on my camp lantern and take out my notebook. I have a lot of catching up to do because today I saw many unbelievable sights.

I cross off the rocks I listed on my "Things to Look For" list, because I found every one—even schist! In fact, my sleeping bag is lying on some very hard schist this minute. On a clean sheet of paper, I write:

THINGS I HAVE FOUND

And under it I put:

1. Cave
2. Jen

Well, Chad really found Jen, then Jen and Chad found us, but I'm putting it here anyway. I close my notebook, then open it and add another thing:

3. Dad

18

CLOUDY, WITH A CHANCE OF TODD

AFTER EXPLORING THE BOTTOM, side, and top of the canyon Sunday and Monday, I'm ready to leave this place. I still think it has the most beautiful rocks I've ever seen, but today they look more boring than before. Mom is tired. And Jen is in a bad mood since she decided Chad is not much fun. When we went fishing in the river, Chad was more interested in the trout than in Jen.

On Tuesday evening, we pull up the driveway and are home. After seeing so many tall cliffs, mountains, and plateaus, our house looks teeny. But I think this house is the best place on Earth. Even better than the Grand Canyon. I'll never forget the Grand Canyon, and I will go back someday. The rangers are wondering when I'm returning that fossil I borrowed, I'm sure.

I take out my science book and look through the last part of our "Rocks and Minerals" chapter. We are almost at the end of our unit, The Living Earth. As I turn the page, I cannot believe what I'm seeing—right there in front of me is a picture of the South Rim. How come I didn't notice this before? I'll have lots to say to the class when we talk about that picture. Mrs. Montemore will be thrilled when I tell every fact I wrote down about rocks, fossils, hiking, and thunderstorms in the canyon. And if we get to the "Weather" chapter this year, Mrs. Montemore will need my cloud notes, too. What would Mrs. Montemore do without an earth scientist in her classroom?

"Sam, Kelli's here," Jen calls from the kitchen."

Jen's been much sweeter to me lately. I'm going to let her borrow my green spiral notebook to study for her science test next week. But she better give it back before I have the same test in ninth grade.

I walk down the hall toward the kitchen. Kelli meets me eight-fourths of the way.

"Sam, you missed so much around here since I talked to you last." Kelli hops up and down so fast that the ruffles on her skirt flap like butterfly wings.

"What?" I ask. "Holy cannoli, Kell. Hold still."

"Somebody moved in next to me yesterday! Guess who!"

"In the Turners' old house?" I ask. "Oh, no. Don't tell me. Did that redheaded, dimple-faced Richard Frey move in there? I don't want That Kid following me around. How am I going to get away from him if he lives on my street?"

"Nope, it's not Richard. Guess again," Kelli says. She grins like she knows a huge secret.

"I don't have a clue," I sigh. "Who?"

"Think really perfect teeth, dark eyes, quiet," Kelli says.

"Todd? Todd is your next-door neighbor? He lives two houses from me?"

Kelli starts hopping again. "Remember I told you he was moving? He didn't move out of the school district. His parents just wanted a bigger place. They moved in yesterday."

I don't know what to say. But I do know that Todd will be my boyfriend someday because I'm going to march over there and ask him.

"Well, anyway," Kelli says, "Todd has to do this scouting project on bugs. He asked me if I wanted to help him stick dead bugs on poster board. *Bor*-ing! Is he out of his mind for asking *me* for help? Bug guts are yellow and green and red! *Eeeww!* Major gross. You don't mind bug guts, Sam. So you should help him. When he comes over to my house tomorrow, I'll give him your number."

Kelli knows I don't mind bugs at all. I have a poster above my bed with a dissected grasshopper on it. It shows every part of its body—the head, thorax, and abdomen. Kelli says that poster is disgusting. I'm glad Kelli's telling Todd I'll help him with the dead bugs. She's a good best friend. Wait. Why is Todd going over to *her* house? Does Kelli want Todd to be her boyfriend someday, too?

I'm thinking that maybe I'll help Todd pretty soon. And I'm thinking that I *ab-so*-lutely need to tell him how much I love bugs. Maybe soon I'll love them even more than rocks.

CHANGE

RIGHT BEFORE I GO TO BED, I peek in Jen's room and toss my notebook on her bed. "Mom says you have a test on rocks soon," I say. "My notes might help."

"Thanks," she says. "I cannot believe we have to study this in high school. My environmental science teacher, Mr. Davids, is making us do an entire geology unit. Ugh, I thought that once we studied it in fourth grade, we were done for good. I don't know how you do it, Sam. You're great with this stuff."

I shrug my shoulders. Jen's not always a pain-in-the-butt big sister.

Jen perches in front of the mirror and twists her hair up in a bun—the spiky kind that I like. Then she turns to me.

"Come here," she says. Jen plops me down where she was sitting. "I'm doing your hair."

"In a cool bun, like yours?" I ask. "But it's time for bed. It'll get ruined."

Jen ignores me and brushes my hair. Hard. I want to scream at her for yanking my head back, but I don't. It actually feels good to have someone brush my hair. And besides, Jen seems like she's having so much fun. In minutes, I have a swirly cinnamon bun on my head, and it sprouts spikes in all the right places.

"You look nice," Jen says.

She sounds exactly like a grown-up. Exactly like Mom. I cross my eyes at her and laugh.

Jen laughs, too, and then gets very serious. "I bet Todd will think you look pretty. I know you like him."

"But he likes Kelli," I sigh. "He hasn't been in this neighborhood for five minutes, and guess what? He's going over to her house.

And then there's Richard—Richard Frey, who called me a science freak on the playground, and who said, 'Samantha Hansen has rocks in her head.' Richard Frey really likes me now, I think. Ever since the talent show. That Kid could end up as my boyfriend someday, *if* Todd doesn't work out."

"Such drama," Jen says. She pulls the elastic hair band out, and my bun flies apart.

"Hey, what are you doing?" I yell. "*Jennn!*"

Jen hands me the brush. "Your turn," she says. "You can do it. And let's keep our voices down so Mom doesn't come in and tell you to get to bed."

Wait. My sister wants me to stay out of trouble?

I pull my hair off my face. Jen whispers hair-fixing directions and moves her hands like a traffic cop. "Left. Go around. Now right. Turn that piece under. Stop there."

I try to do what she says, but my twisted hair ends up looking more like a pig's tail than a cinnamon bun. And the spikes are too short, I'm sure.

"You'll get the hang of it," Jen says. "Maybe another night I can do a complete makeover on you. I'll change your hair, your outfit. I can even change your face with some makeup."

I give Jen a good-night hug. "OK," I say.

But I'm *ab-so*-lutely not letting her change me anytime soon.

Coming soon: Nancy Viau's next book,

SOMETHING IS BUGGING SAMANTHA HANSEN

1

NO MORE ROCKS IN MY HEAD

IT'S BEEN MONTHS since our Grand Canyon trip. I miss that place. I miss the rainbow plateaus, the huge chunks of sedimentary rock, and the fossils. That Grand Canyon trip was a dream come true for a scientist like me. But my dream turned into a nightmare when I found out that my best friend, Kelli, tried to steal my future boyfriend!

It started last fall on our class trip to Slippery Stone Cave. I was being extremely helpful to our cave guide, Susie, and That Kid Richard Frey said I was a science freak and had rocks in my head. But Todd Kensington stuck up for me. He wanted me to say more cave facts, all the while showing off his perfectly white teeth. I decided right then and there that Todd would be my boyfriend one day—one day in a few years when I was allowed to have a boyfriend. I would ask him to go to museums and on dates. My older sister, Jen, goes on dates with her boyfriend, Timmy. Dates seem like a lot of work because you have to wear make-up. I don't like that part much.

But then Kelli invited Todd over to her house, and I got to thinking . . . maybe Kelli wants Todd for a boyfriend. Good thing Todd never made it over there. But still, I got *so* mad at Kelli.

Kelli and I don't stay mad for long. She's been my friend since kindergarten. Best friend. I've only gotten mad at her ten or fifty times since we met.

Kelli used to spend tons of time over at my house. But since we started back to school after Christmas vacation, she's only been over twice. I am calling her right this minute to find out why.

Kelli answers after only one ring. She has a cell phone now and never misses a call. I want a cell phone too, but Mom says "maybe later." When she says that, it means "no."

"Hi, Sam," Kelli says. "What's up?"

I'm surprised Kelli knows it's me. Then I remember. Cell phones tell you who's calling because your name pops up. "Wanna come over, Kell? Or I could come over there? Your swing set needs some exercise."

Kelli starts yakking away. "I can't. I'm taking a ballet class. It's in an hour, and my tutu is nowhere! Tutus are required. My ballet teacher, Miss Kim, says so. I cannot miss class. I'm already months behind because I didn't start until two weeks ago. We are working on third position tonight. Ling says my first position is very good, and my second position is better than average. I can't wait to be really good at first, second, third, fourth, and fifth. Just like Ling. She slides into those positions like a prima ballerina. Ling says that if I practice, the positions will get easier and easier. So, I'm signed up to go every Monday, Wednesday, and Friday. And guess what? Ling is at the studio on the same days. Ling says . . ."

Kelli goes on and on with three more sentences that begin with "Ling says." I get it. Kelli and Ling are ballet dancers, together. Kelli used to be an Irish step dancer. She did that for the talent show. And *only* Ling did ballet. But now Kelli does it, too? Sounds like she's ballet-ing with Ling a lot. And they're spending lots of after-school time together.

"And there will be a recital in May," Kelli says. "Ling and I dance . . ."

I blow a loud sigh into the phone. *Pshoo!* I'm not really listening. My ears are broken from the Ling-a-ringing. I *ab-so-*lutely want to scream. But I don't because I have learned to calm myself down.

Sort of.

Not really.

I count to ten, whispering under my breath. "One, two, three, four, five, six, seven-eight-nine-ten." I hurry through the last part because this counting stuff doesn't work as great as it used to.

Kelli has not stopped talking. "And then Ling said . . ."

I try some Spanish counting. "*Uno, dos, tres . . .*" Wait. What comes next . . . *cinco?* A little louder, I say, "*Uno, dos, tres*, something, *cinco*, *seis,* something . . ."

"Did you talk in Spanish?" Kelli asks. "Ling's mom is from Puerto Rico, and she—"

I cut Kelli off. "Holy guacamole, Kell! I've got to run. I think my mom is calling me." Mom is not calling me, but she could be. It's almost time for dinner. I tell Kelli I'll see her in school tomorrow and hang up.

Something is *really* bugging me. Big time. It's a thought that's sitting on my brain like a teeny fly. No, not like a fly. More like a chubby slug. Maybe I didn't hear straight, but it sounds like Kelli and Ling are best friends now. *I am* Kelli's best friend, not Ling. Oh, no! Do I need a new best friend?

My mad thoughts are exploding in my brain. And those explosions are wiggling their way to my feet. I ram my foot into the floor once. *Stomp!* Then twice. *Stomp! Stomp!* Then, with very heavy steps, I run in circles around the living room. And down the hall, really fast—*stompitystompstomp!* I add one more super-duper loud stomp just because. *STOMP!*

I am definitely not ballet material.

OTHER SCHIFFER BOOKS FROM THIS AUTHOR

BEAUTY AND BERNICE

Bernice is the only girl at the skate park who can pop an ollie and ride the rails. She'd love to impress Wyatt, another skater, but needs help from her new neighbor, the proper and princessy Odelia. This adventurous novel asks the question: Can two very different people be friends?

JUST ONE THING!

Anthony Pantaloni needs Just One Thing!—one thing he does well, one thing that will replace the Antsy Pants nickname he got tagged with on the first day of fifth grade, one good thing he can "own" before moving up to middle school next year.

ABOUT THE AUTHOR

Nancy Viau's love of travel has taken her to many of America's national parks, but she counts the Grand Canyon—stinky burros and all—as her favorite. *Samantha Hansen Has Rocks in Her Head* was inspired by a family trip to Arizona. (She promises that one day, she will travel back to Grand Canyon National Park and return the rock she "borrowed.") Viau has worked as an elementary school teacher, an instructor for reluctant readers, a counselor in an after-school program, and a freelance writer. Her other middle-grade novels include *Something is Bugging Samantha Hansen*, *Beauty and Bernice*, and *Just One Thing!* Please visit www.NancyViau.com for information on these titles and her picture books.